"Wednesday afternoon they're having tryouts for the orchestra," Dennis said to me. "Promise you'll come—and bring your violin!"

Did I imagine a tiny twinge of envy on Melissa's perfect face? Perhaps that look was what made me bold enough to say, "I might. I'm not sure. I told you I don't play in public."

Dennis's hand was on my shoulder. "Well, we're all pushing, Elizabeth. Wednesday. Promise?"

"OK, I promise."

"I'll see you there," Dennis said, his voice stern. He gave my shoulder a little squeeze.

All afternoon long, the memory of that warm, strong hand on my shoulder remained with me. It even blocked out—almost—the memory of Melissa Cooper's pretty, sophisticated face.

Bantam Sweet Dreams Romances
Ask your bookseller for the books you have missed

Love Song

Anne Park

BANTAM BOOKS
TORONTO · NEW YORK · LONDON · SYDNEY

RL 5, IL age 11 and up

LOVE SONG
A Bantam Book / August 1982

ISBN 0-553-22542-1

Published simultaneously in the United States and Canada

Bantam Books are published by Bantam Books, Inc. Its trademark, consisting of
the words ''Bantam Books'' and the portrayal of a rooster, is Registered in U.S.
Patent and Trademark Office and in other countries. Marca Registrada. Bantam
Books, Inc., 666 Fifth Avenue, New York, New York 10103.

PRINTED IN THE UNITED STATES OF AMERICA

O   0 9 8 7 6 5 4 3 2 1

Love Song

Chapter One

Walking two inches above the sidewalk because Dennis Whitcomb had asked me for a date, I turned the corner onto our street and floated down the block. My beautiful mood evaporated, however, when I reached our house. Seeing it, a small, discouraged-looking cottage with its white paint flaking off, I was brought back to reality. Dennis was an only child of affluent parents, and he lived on East Boulevard. Hawkins Street and East Boulevard may be only two miles apart, but in our small city in upstate New York, the distance is just about the same as that between Buckingham Palace and a London slum.

Opening the front door, I shouted, "I'm home!" But no one answered. From the den I could hear the clatter of typewriter keys; from the kitchen came the pungent smell of burning meat. I went there first.

1

On the back burner of our ancient gas stove sat the big soup kettle, and in it, boiled dry, was a beef soup bone. I turned off the jet, found a ragged potholder, and jerked the kettle off the stove into the sink. I ran a little water into the pot, and steam boiled up into my face.

"Ugh!" The odor of scorched meat was overpowering, and I knew the soup bone couldn't be salvaged. My mother's famous vegetable soup would taste only like burned meat.

Prentice, our dog, was peering hopefully through the screen door, his tongue hanging out. "Don't worry," I said. "It's as good as yours."

I filled the teakettle and set it over the front burner, opened the door for the five cats, who seemed to have materialized from nowhere, and shook some Kat Kernels into their dishes. They all began to eat, lined up like a cat food commercial, their tails in the air. Prentice, who is part spaniel and part airedale, pushed his way in so that he could eat from one of the dishes. No one has ever told him he's not a cat.

I knocked on the door of the den, and my mother said, "Come in."

When I entered, she was still facing the typewriter. She was perched on a wooden kitchen chair with a pillow for a cushion. "After I sit for an hour or two, my bum begins to hurt," she always says.

Her hair, red gold and thick, caught up in an untidy mass in the back, was stabbed through with a ball-point pen. Her old, blue cotton blouse had a rip under the sleeve. She turned around and smiled at me, a wide, dazzling smile, as though I were the person in the world she wanted most to see.

"Elizabeth! Are you home from school already?"

I went over and kissed her cheek. "It's nearly four-thirty, Mother, and the soup boiled away. What'll we have for dinner?"

She looked conscience stricken. "I thought I smelled something, but I wanted to finish typing the last two pages of my story. I honestly forgot, Elizabeth. Oh, dear, that soup bone cost almost two dollars. That's sinful." She sighed. "I guess we'll have to have eggs." Then she brightened. "I'll make cheese strata. Everyone likes that."

"That'll be great. Want a cup of tea?"

She stretched her arms above her head. "Sure. I need a break."

My mother writes confession stories for magazines. My father died five years ago, when I was eleven, and since then, my mother has earned a living that way. When Daddy was alive, story sales were always cause for great celebration, and the money went to buy little luxuries or Christmas gifts, or it paid for vacations. Now the sales, combined with what we get from Social Security, pay the bills. My mother is a very smart woman. Before she and my father were

3

married, she had a career in advertising, but she likes her writing better.

"I like to work at home so that I can keep an eye on you children," she always says. Actually, I feel as though I've been keeping an eye on her lately. If I'd been home, the soup bone would never have burned.

I went back to the kitchen and made us each a mug of tea. There were cookies, full of nutmeg and dates, the kind we all like. She must have baked them before she started writing that morning. I decided not to resist them, since dinner wouldn't be all that exciting.

When I went back to the den, my mother was stretched out on the old, blue studio couch, hands behind her head, ready to talk to me—ready, I knew, to give me her undivided attention. She sipped the tea and ate a cookie.

"Well," she said finally, "how was your day?"

I could feel the smile splitting the corners of my mouth. "Dennis Whitcomb asked me for a date Friday night." It was not a casual statement, and she knew it.

"Elizabeth! That's wonderful. I knew he would, of course, but I didn't know *when*."

"Oh, Mother, you're such an optimist. *I* didn't think he ever would. He dates people like Melissa Cooper and Dusty Carter. They're all popular and sort of rich—and they're part of his crowd."

My mother gave me a severe look. "Just remember that you're as good as any of them,

Elizabeth. I think it might have been Artur Rubenstein, who, when asked by customs if he had anything to declare, said, 'I have nothing to declare but my talent.' You have talent, and if you develop it, that will be your entrée into any circle you choose."

I shied away from that. My violin and I have a special relationship, but I knew I'd never be a truly great musician because I wasn't prepared to sacrifice everything for it, as my father had. He taught me to play, and Uncle Bob, Daddy's brother, has given me lessons since my father died. Uncle Bob is a good teacher, but the violin is his hobby, not his vocation. He says he needs a paycheck at the end of every week. I've always felt I'm more like him than I am like my parents.

While we were drinking our tea, the front door slammed, and Justin came into the den. "Hi. What's for dinner? I hope it's not whatever I smell in the kitchen. Something stinks."

Michelle, who is twelve, and Bonita, who is eight, look alike: tall, slender, with delicate, heart-shaped faces framed by curly, red gold hair like Mother's. Justin, who is ten, and I look alike. We both have oval faces, straight, yellow hair, and wide smiles. Justin hates looking like me.

"The soup bone burned," Mother said. "We're having cheese strata. Have two cookies and a glass of milk. Everything go all right today?"

"Everything's fine." Things usually are fine

with Justin. He takes life as it comes. "Where are Shell and Bonnie?"

"Michelle and Bonita," Mother said pointedly, "are doing Michelle's paper route. They should be home soon."

Mother always calls us by our full names. She says she likes our given names, otherwise she would have named us Bonnie and Shell and Liz. And we were taught to call her Mother, not Mom.

Justin said nothing, just went dashing off to the kitchen. It's a sore point with him that Michelle, a girl, is old enough to have a paper route, while he has nearly two years to wait.

I took a last swallow of tea. "Guess I'll go practice my fiddle for an hour before dinner," I said. "I have a lot of homework to do tonight."

Mother smiled at me. "I'm so glad about the date with Dennis, sweetie. Amy know about it?"

"I'm going to call her right after dinner. She had Science Club this afternoon."

I went upstairs to my room. All the bedrooms are tiny. Mother has one; Justin has the smallest; Michelle and Bonita share one; and I have the attic room. As always when I entered it, I felt a sense of peace and happiness. It is a pretty room with wooden beams and slanted ceilings that have been papered in a blue-sprigged wallpaper. The bed is set between two dormered windows, and my white-painted bookcase and secondhand stereo, paid for out of baby-sitting money, are opposite. And my music stand, of course. Here I can practice the violin all I want to, without bothering anybody.

"Elizabeth, you and I are the musical ones," Daddy used to say. "Your mother and Justin are the writers. Michelle is going to be the first woman president of the USA. It remains to be seen where Bonita's talents lie." Bonita was only three when Daddy died of a heart attack.

I opened my windows and knelt on the bed for a few moments, looking out at the back yard. The grass was still lush and green, and there were flowers blooming, but Indian summer was nearly there. A few zucchini and yellow summer squash lay among the drying leaves in the little vegetable garden. The air smelled wonderful, a pungent blend of summer and fall. It smelled like Mozart or perhaps like Strauss. Wolfgang Amadeus Mozart. Johann Strauss the younger. It wasn't a day for scales, nor for practicing my fingering. It was a day for the "Blue Danube," for love songs, for Dennis.

I took the violin tenderly from its case—Daddy's violin—and tucked it under my chin, cradling it as I had seen him do so many times. I thought of Dennis with his light brown hair and his white teeth, so dazzling against his tanned face, so heartwarming when he smiled. He had the smile of Robert Redford, sudden, unexpected, completely captivating. And today he had smiled at me, Elizabeth Ashton! I still couldn't believe it.

I felt as though only Strauss could express my feelings, so I played through the "Blue Danube" and "Voices of Spring" and "Artist's Life." When I finally stopped, I looked out the window again, and there was my mother, sitting on a wooden lawn chair in the back yard. Figaro, the big gray tomcat, sat beside her, like a guardian, like a sacred cat guarding a queen in an old Egyptian wall painting. I knew they had been listening to my mini-concert. I knew, too, that they were audience enough for me; I didn't need to perform for outsiders.

Something had been nagging at me, though, and as I put the violin in its case, I realized what it was. If Dennis picked me up Friday night, he'd have to come here, to this shabby, cluttered, little house with the sofa that desperately needs a slipcover and the woodwork that needs paint. He'd be met by the kids—I hadn't had many dates, and they'd be curious—by Prentice, whose favorite bed was the big living room chair, and by an assortment of cats who shed their hair indiscriminately on furniture and people.

When I called Amy, I decided I would ask if she and Kevin would like to double-date with Dennis and me. Then I'd think of a reason for Dennis to pick me up at Amy's house. But I knew that if he asked me out again, he'd have to see me as I really was.

I pushed the thought away and ran downstairs to help with dinner.

Chapter Two

I was heading toward the kitchen, my mouth all set for the cheese strata and chef's salad, when I heard voices from the living room. Aunt Carolyn and Uncle Bob. I adore Uncle Bob, who is a taller, sandier, heavier version of my father. Aunt Carolyn is also very tall, with dark, perfectly groomed hair and a severely attractive face. She is the sort of person who looks at the seams of homemade dresses, but she's very kind in her own way. Uncle Bob and Aunt Carolyn have no children, and they've been very good to us Ashtons, buying us winter coats at Christmas and paying an occasional dentist's bill.

I went in and said hello. Prentice was leaning against Uncle Bob's pant leg and Thomas, our yellow cat, was sitting on Aunt Carolyn's lap. I plucked him off. She was wearing a navy blue suit, and I didn't think she'd like it decorated with yellow fur. Besides, I have the feeling that she's really afraid of animals.

"We could hear your violin as we came up the walk," she said. "It was lovely, Elizabeth, just lovely."

Every time Uncle Bob speaks, I remember my father. Uncle Bob's voice is so similar to my dad's, so full of gentleness and humor. "You're good, honey. I think you're about due to have a more proficient teacher than your old uncle." I thought he looked a little sad as he added, "You might think of a professional career—sort of do it for the Old Gipper."

I kissed the top of his head, where the sandy hair was thinning. "You know I'm too much like you, Uncle Bob. I don't like the idea of starving in a garret, or wherever it is musicians starve."

Aunt Carolyn nodded approvingly, but my mother frowned. She's always lecturing me about the parable of the talents in the Bible. "Even if your talent is small," she always says, "you must develop it, in gratitude for the gift you've been given."

Now she said, "I hope you two will stay for dinner—no, it's supper tonight. Cheese strata and salad and dessert. How does that sound?"

Uncle Bob looked eager, but Aunt Carolyn's rather long, thin nose wrinkled just a bit, and I knew she could still smell the scorched soup bone. "Our dinner is all prepared," she said.

11

"We're having a cold meal tonight." Then she added curiously, "What is cheese strata?"

"Oh, it's eggs and bread and cheese and milk baked together. It's really good, Carolyn, and very nourishing." She looked impish and added, "It's fortunate that the children love it because I burned the soup bone I'd planned to use tonight."

The others came trooping in to say hello, and pretty soon Aunt Carolyn stood up to go. When I looked at the house through her eyes, I could see shabbiness everywhere. And I knew Dennis's eyes wouldn't be so different from hers. It wasn't that I thought them supercritical; it's just that, when you have money and comforts, I'm sure you think everyone else has.

As they were leaving, Mother said, "Thank you again for the clothes, Carolyn. Michelle is so tall, it won't take much doing to alter them for her."

I felt a flash of helpless fury. Aunt Carolyn bought beautiful, expensive clothing, but the dresses were too mature looking for my sister Michelle, who deserves things bought for her delicate prettiness, not for a middle-aged woman.

When they had left, we gathered around the dining room table to eat our cheese strata off the blue-and-white willowware—a bequest from Grandma Ashton. I looked around, trying to see my family as Dennis would.

Bonita, at eight, was beginning to thin out,

her legs a little gangly, her elbows sharp, her brown eyes enormous in her tanned, little face. Justin was shoveling the food in methodically, merely stoking the furnace, his mind on other matters, I suppose. That's why Daddy figured him for a writer even when he was only four or five. Even then he'd had a big imagination and a laid-back approach to life, as though he were studying people without judging them.

When Mother asked Bonita why she wasn't eating, Bonita said, "I don't like cheese much anymore. I'd rather have a hamburger at Mc-Donald's or Burger King."

"Tonight," Mother said, "cheese is what we're having. Be thankful. We'll go out for hamburgers on your birthday."

To Michelle she said, "Aunt Carolyn brought a big box of clothes. You can look them over after dinner and see what you like. They're your size."

Michelle scowled at Mother. "They might be my size, but I'll bet they're not my style." She looked haughty. "I can buy clothes out of my route money."

Mother is unexpectedly practical about things like this. "Waste not, want not," she said firmly. "You can save your newspaper money for your education."

"I hate hand-me-downs," Michelle said. "They never feel right."

I said, "How could they? You're nothing like Aunt Carolyn, except in height."

I felt sorry when I saw how sad Mother looked. Then she brightened and said, "If I sell my novel, I promise it will be new things all around for everyone—including new slipcovers for the living room furniture."

Michelle said sullenly, "If you ever finish it, you might sell it, but you're always too busy writing those dumb confessions."

Justin took a swallow of milk. "I have faith in you, Mother." He looked so loving and so sincere that I dropped a kiss on his blond head as I went toward the kitchen with a stack of plates.

"We all have faith in you," I said, when I brought the fruit and homemade cookies back to the table. "The book's nearly finished, isn't it?"

She looked so young and so pretty in the candlelight. She really is an interesting person, I thought. I wouldn't trade her for anyone's mother.

"About fifty pages to go," she said, the corners of her mouth turning up irresistibly—a habit we have in common.

"Dibs on the phone," I said, grabbing a handful of cookies and a plum. "I have to call Amy. "It's your turn to do the dishes, Michelle."

I sat on the fourth stair step, pulled the phone through the railing onto my lap, and dialed.

She answered on the second ring. "Amy? It's me."

I could picture her, small and dark haired and pretty, stretched out on her bed, ready to talk for ages. Amy is such a good friend. Although she's a very practical person herself, she understands people like me, people who have their ups and downs, their uncertainties. It's a very comforting feeling, having Amy for a friend.

I had meant to be very nonchalant about it, but instead I blurted it out almost immediately. "Amy, Dennis Whitcomb asked me for a date Friday night!"

"Lizbeth! That's marvelous! When did he ask you? Where?"

"I was in the library after school, looking up some stuff for that miserable history paper. I was sitting there reading, taking notes on ancient Rome, and Dennis sat down across the table from me."

Pausing for dramatic effect, I savored that moment in the sunny, book-scented library. When Dennis had slid into the chair opposite me, I'd scarcely dared look up. But finally I'd glanced over at him and smiled tentatively.

"Well, go on," Amy said. "What happened next?"

So I told her that we'd started to talk about our notes for our papers—although he's a senior and I'm a junior, we're both in Miss Yancey's class. Then we talked about a movie we'd both seen, and before I knew it, he was asking me out.

After Amy and I had talked about Dennis's gorgeous smile and how good he was at basketball and soccer and acting, I said, trying to be sensible, "I know that I'm only one of several, of course. He dates lots of girls." That reminded me. "They're all so much *richer* than I am, Amy. Cindy's father's a judge, and Melissa Cooper's father is a doctor. And both of Dennis's parents are lawyers." I tried to laugh. "I'm just a poor little orphan."

Amy doesn't worry about things like that. She could be rich or poor, instead of just in-between, and she wouldn't care either way. She's just Amy.

"Don't worry so much, Liz. You're pretty, and you're interesting, and you're talented. What more do you want?"

A different background, I wanted to say. Besides, I had grave doubts about all those other attributes; she's my best friend and prejudiced. But instead, I brought up the subject of double-dating, and she was enthusiastic.

"Sure, why not? You can tell Dennis you're invited to supper at my house—and you are, you know—and the boys can pick us up here."

After that we talked about other things that had happened at school that day, and finally we hung up.

16

I got to my feet, ready to go upstairs and do my homework, when the phone rang. It was Dennis. After the first thrill of hearing his voice, I felt my heart sink. I'd known it was too good to be true! He'd called to cancel our date.

But what he said was, "Are you busy? We really just got started talking in the library this afternoon."

He was so easy to talk to, not awkward like the few other boys I'd dated. I hadn't been exactly swamped with invitations from boys, and the ones I had gone out with seemed very young beside Dennis.

We talked for a long time about everything: our teachers, friends, the basketball team, which he is on, books, movies, music. It was as though I'd been waiting for sixteen years to find a boy who thought as I did, laughed over the same things, loved Woody Allen, had a passion for cherry vanilla ice cream, and admired Eudora Welty's short stories. Even Amy, with whom I'd been friends since we were four, didn't share all the same tastes. She always says, "Eudora *Who*?"

When we hung up, I ran up the two flights of stairs to my attic room. I didn't want anyone, even Mother, to intrude on my thoughts just then. They were too beautiful, too tender, too . . . uncertain, I suppose.

In the dark, I knelt on the bed and looked out into the moonlit night. The soft breeze stirred

17

the curtains and my hair. At this beautiful, dreamy moment, I could forget all my worries about Dennis and Melissa Cooper and Dusty Carter. I could forget that he might feel sorry for our struggling family. He really likes me! I thought. This has been the happiest day of my life! Dennis Whitcomb likes me.

Chapter Three

The next morning, however, I didn't feel so optimistic. I got up late because I had been holding imaginary conversations with Dennis half the night, and I felt dull from lack of sleep. Cranky, too. Last night, after my long telephone talk with Dennis, the world had seemed so beautiful, so full of promise, but this morning I was seeing the world—my world, at least—for what it was. And it was dull and unglamorous and sometimes very difficult.

Justin attends the World of Inquiry School for gifted students, and he has to catch the bus at eight o'clock. At seven-forty-five he was still sitting at the breakfast table, dreamily spooning cereal into his mouth.

"See if you can push him along a little," Mother said, quietly despairing. "I wish I knew what makes that boy tick."

I shook him none too gently. "Justin, finish that cereal this minute!"

He sighed, but he began to cram the soggy cornflakes into his mouth.

"That's the way to do it," I said to my mother. "You're too nice to him."

She lifted her eyebrows. "I thought you were over the moon with happiness last night, and now you sound pretty edgy. What's wrong?"

I shrugged. "I don't want to talk about it. Let's get this slowpoke off to school."

Justin wiped his mouth hastily, tossed the crumpled paper napkin into the wastebasket, missing by a foot, ran a hand through his tousled hair, kissed Mother, and made a dash for the front door. Prentice followed, barking excitedly, and I saw Justin chase him back, just as the yellow school bus pulled up in front of the house. When I saw him waving from the bus window, I couldn't help smiling at him. He looked like a little English schoolboy with his rounded, rosy cheeks and his straight, yellow hair. It was hard to stay angry with Justin for very long because he was never irritating on purpose; he was simply a dreamer.

Back in the kitchen, Mother poured herself a cup of coffee and sat down at the kitchen table, resting her elbows on the yellow-painted, round wooden table.

"Get some breakfast and join me," she said.

"You don't have to be at school until ten today, right?"

Michelle and Bonita, who walk to school together—Bonita to elementary school, Michelle to the Middle School—had set their breakfast dishes in the sink and had wiped up the counters. I added Justin's bowl and glass to theirs, poured myself some orange juice and popped an English muffin into the toaster. Mother said very little, but I saw her watching me as I buttered the muffin and spread homemade strawberry jam on it. I ate it slowly and then made myself a cup of tea.

Before I drank the tea, I got the aspirin bottle from the cupboard where it had been kept since I was little, out of reach of small kids.

"Headache, dear?" Mother asked solicitously.

"No, I just take these because I like the taste," I said, then felt guilty for being so sarcastic. "I didn't sleep well, and my head feels like cotton."

Mother doesn't encourage us to take any kind of medicine, but she said, "Well, sip the tea. Between that and the aspirin, you should feel better by the time you leave."

Drinking her coffee slowly, she waited, not even glancing at the morning paper that was beside her. She wouldn't push; she never does. But I knew that she was expecting me to tell her what was bothering me.

Groping for words, I looked around me. The kitchen didn't look bad this morning, with the

21

September sunlight filtering through the white curtains over the sink and shining on the copper kettle I'd given Mother for her birthday. It wasn't bad, but it was nothing like Amy's family kitchen, all modern with built-in appliances. I was surprised at how much I wanted a home like Amy's.

It was partly, of course, for my mother's sake. She deserved something better. But today, I knew, it was mostly because of Dennis Whitcomb. I couldn't picture him sitting at the old wooden kitchen table, looking down at the worn, cracked linoleum. All night long, as I'd tossed and turned, I'd thought about the possibility that Dennis might come here, and knew I couldn't face it. One talk in the library, one long telephone conversation, one upcoming date, and I seemed to have changed from a moderately content sixteen-year-old to someone aware of the possibilities of a better, more affluent life.

"Mother—" I said finally, drinking up the last of the tea and feeling the headache begin to lift a little. I sat there, searching for words.

"What's on your mind?" she asked quietly. I had the feeling she was expecting an outburst, and I tried to keep it down.

"I know we're living on Social Security and on your writing, and I'm old enough to know what a struggle you're having, but you could change things if you wanted to."

"How do you mean?"

I had the feeling this was coming out all wrong, but I plunged in anyway.

"You're smart, Mother, and very creative, but it's pretty hard to make a living being creative. You need a job with a salary at the end of the week, so we can live like human beings."

She had become very quiet, but she seemed determined to hear me out. Her face looked pinched and white, and I began to wish I hadn't started.

"Why can't you borrow money and go back to college and get your degree? That's what Amy's mother did, and that's how she became a teacher, and now they can have two cars and take trips and enjoy life."

Mother looked stricken. "And all along, I thought we *were* enjoying life."

That made me ashamed. "Well, we do, of course. We have lots of fun, you know that. But everything is so *difficult,* Mother. If we go to a movie, we take our own popcorn, because it's too expensive to buy it in the theater. Michelle wears Aunt Carolyn's made-over clothes, and I feel guilty when I use my baby-sitting money to buy a pair of jeans—in the bargain basement at Talbot's."

Mother was studying me. "I'm not sure I would do much differently, even if we had plenty of money. I'm not in favor of giving children everything. That takes the joy out of earning it."

I sighed and muttered sulkily, "A few luxuries wouldn't spoil us. Like some new furniture. And a car so that we could go on a vacation once in awhile. Everyone I know takes those things for granted."

She got up, took our dishes to the sink, filled the sink with hot water, and poured in the detergent before she answered me. "Elizabeth, when your father died, I weighed things carefully and decided I'd scrimp along on the Social Security for you children and my confession stories. That way, I could stay home with you. It was my choice. It may have been the wrong one, in your eyes, but it was right for me. And I think it was right for the younger children, at least."

She turned around and looked at me, and I could see tears in her green eyes. "I don't really care about a degree because I don't want to be a teacher nor an account executive in an advertising agency. I want to do what I'm doing because it makes me happy."

Why was I so angry with her? I jumped up from my chair, snatched up my books and sweater, and said, "Happiness isn't everything, Mother."

I gave her a kiss on the cheek, which was more like a bite, said goodbye, and left.

Perhaps I'd had a premonition that I wouldn't have a really great day, because I didn't. My first class was French, and I realized I'd forgotten my homework paper, which wouldn't exactly endear me to Mlle La Rue. The homework was neatly done, too, and I was furious with myself. I remembered leaving it on my dresser, planning to put it in my notebook, but I'd forgotten it completely. Mlle La Rue, who comes from Paris, never takes excuses. Either you have your work done or you receive an E for that day's work. My record had been so good, too.

I was right. She didn't accept my excuse. "The eye must see the work, *n'est-ce pas*?" Her little black eyes regarded me reproachfully. "You are such a reliable student, Elizabeth, I am sorry to have to consider your homework undone."

Amy waited for me outside the classroom door. "Have you seen Dennis yet?" I shook my head. "I saw him in homeroom. He really is gorgeous, Lizbeth. That smile! I think that's what makes him so good-looking, that and that dark blond hair."

I began to feel better. Why was I looking for trouble? After all, Dennis had asked me for a date. That meant he liked me, didn't it? We were going out Friday night. What more could I ask?

Amy and I went into the lunchroom together at noon, and I looked around the room quickly, hoping to see Dennis. It was crowded—this was the first lunch hour—and at first I couldn't spot him. When I did see him, I wished I hadn't.

25

He was sitting at a table with Bat Saunders and two girls whom I knew only by sight. He and Bat seemed to be having a great time, laughing and talking with the girls.

Amy saw them, too. Good old Amy. She grabbed her tray and started to steer me toward the far corner, where Ginny Bond and Cindy Grant were saving us seats. "Come on," she said, "I'm starving." Then she looked down at her plate of watery chow mein and Chinese noodles. "I'd *have* to be starving to eat this glop."

I laughed and pretended I hadn't seen Dennis and his friends. Common sense told me he'd had friends of both sexes before he asked me out, and he'd have those same friends today and tomorrow. But I couldn't help wishing he had noticed me in the lunchroom or had looked for me, at least.

All in all, it was a bad day, and I guess, when you come right down to it, most of it was my own fault. I'd gotten out of bed "on the wrong side," as my grandfather used to say, and I'd continued on the wrong side all day. I really felt let down about Dennis, about whom I'd been fantasizing ever since he'd asked me out. But most of all, I felt really mean for fighting with my mother. No way could our life style measure up to Dennis Whitcomb's family's style, at least not in the conceivable future, and it was cruel of me to upset my mother that way.

When I got home from school that afternoon, I did make myself apologize to my mother. She was generous about it; she always is. But I thought there was a kind of sad look about her eyes, so that they looked more gray than green, and all of a sudden, I saw tiny lines around her mouth, lines I hadn't ever noticed. It was as though my harsh words had aged her by making her more aware of unhappiness. I felt as though I'd ripped away the veil through which my romantic mother looked at life.

I didn't talk to Amy very long after dinner that night. For one thing, I was too gloomy to say very much, and for another, I kept hoping Dennis might call me. He didn't. And that made me wonder whether or not our date was on for the next night. Wednesday night he had seemed so warm and friendly, so interested in everything about me. I'd been sure he liked me almost as much as I liked him, but perhaps I was just a dreamer, too, like most of my family.

I was as down as I'd been up the night before. "The creative temperament," Mother would call it, but I fought that label. I didn't *want* to have an artistic temperament. I had decided I wanted to be like Uncle Bob—have a job with a paycheck at the end of the week and enjoy my violin as a hobby. It didn't pay to get carried away by your talent, for it might not be enough

27

talent, or the wrong kind of talent, or . . . something. Perhaps I just knew I didn't have my parents' courage, courage to keep going when things are tight and frightening, when it looks as though you might never make it.

Finally I went upstairs to do my homework, but I left the door open so that I could hear the phone if it rang. The heat of the day lingered in my attic room, and I opened the two dormer windows so that the fresh air could enter. Deliberately I chose noisy rock music to put on my stereo. No Mozart or Strauss tonight. I needed something loud and stimulating.

Switching on the lamp, I sat down at my desk, which is only a white-painted wooden table, to do my homework. The French paper was still on my dresser, where it had done me absolutely no good. Dennis and I had the same history class on Mondays, Wednesdays, and Fridays, and I didn't intend to be embarrassed there, as I'd been in French class. Dennis, despite all his extracurricular activities, was a good student. Well, so was I a good student! I would hold up my end in one department, at least.

While I sat there, writing about the wonders of Pompeii, I kept thinking of Dennis. Had Amy's boyfriend, Kevin, gotten in touch with Dennis to tell him they'd pick both of us up at Amy's house? Would he be angry because I'd arranged a double date without asking him? Would he believe that I'd promised to have dinner with Amy; would he think I was afraid to go out alone with him? I hoped not, but Amy was so diplomatic, I could depend on her tact. I completed my homework, then turned off the stereo and went downstairs to our one old-fashioned bathroom to wash my face before going to bed. It was a quarter past eleven, too late to hope for a call from Dennis.

From the bathroom, I could hear Mother's typewriter going, and after I was ready for bed, I went and tapped at the den door. She called, "Come in," and turned to smile at me when I poked my head in the door.

"Those pink pajamas are adorable on you," she said. "Homework all done?"

I nodded. "We had to write on some phase of Pompeii, so I chose the plumbing. It really is wonderful, when you think of it, to know they had all those sewer pipes and things, way back then. And to think it's all been sort of frozen in time by the lava."

She said dryly, "Sewer pipes don't sound too appealing, but I know what you mean. Their civilization was so advanced, all those centuries ago. And we think *we're* so smart."

"I didn't mean to interrupt your work," I told her. "I won't stay long, I promise. Are you working on your novel?"

She nodded. In the daytime she works on the confession stories, which provide an income,

29

but at night, after the younger children are in bed, she usually works on her book. Occasionally she lets me read a few pages of it—a modern novel of marriage and divorce—and I think it's great. If only she had more time to work on it. I'm dying to see it in print. By Eleanor Ashton. My mother.

"Did you talk to Dennis today?"

I shook my head. "No, and I'm wondering if our date is still on. You know I'm going to have dinner at Amy's first, then she and Kevin and Dennis and I are supposed to go out together."

"I'm sure it's still on," she said comfortingly. "Why shouldn't it be?"

"Oh, I don't know. He has so many girls after him."

She smiled, looking young and pretty in the lamplight. "None as wonderful as my daughter! Besides, you're not after him, he's after you."

I didn't tell her how I wished I'd had the courage to call Dennis during the evening, just for reassurance. I'll bet any girl in his crowd wouldn't have thought twice about calling him, but I'm just not the type to telephone a boy. I don't have that kind of easy confidence. Some girls seem to be born with it, but I came equipped with a fair amount of shyness.

"Want me to make you a cup of tea or hot chocolate before I go to bed?"

She shook her head. "I'm fine, dear. I'll probably go to bed and read for a while. And you'd

30

better get some sleep. You have to be up early in the morning."

Back upstairs, I turned out my lamp and crawled into bed. As I lay there, thinking of Dennis, I finally realized what had been bothering me, somewhere in the back of my mind. I hadn't practiced my violin for even twenty minutes today, and that was some kind of record. Even though my lessons came from Uncle Bob, and he wasn't a very hard taskmaster, I always practiced faithfully, every single day, and that included weekends. Because it wasn't just practice and self-discipline. I loved my fiddle, and the music I played on it expressed something deep inside me, something too deep for words. I *needed* that violin.

In the dark, although my fiddle was in its case, I began to practice the fingering of "Liebestraum." Love's dream. Love's dream.

Chapter Four

I saw Dennis in Miss Yancey's history class the next day. We were both two or three minutes early, and he came over to my desk for a minute. He smiled down at me, that fantastic, fatally attractive smile of his, and I melted.

"I hear we're going to meet at Amy Boland's house," he said. "Kevin Murphy called me. He's going to pick me up about eight tonight, and then we'll come for you two girls."

"I hope you don't mind. I'm invited to dinner at Amy's." Which was true, but I didn't tell him it was after the fact. It wouldn't matter, anyway, because he'd probably never ask me out again.

"Kevin thought it might be fun to see that old Woody Allen movie at the university, then we could go dancing or something."

"It sounds like fun!"

Just then Miss Yancey came in and thumped

32

a stack of books and notebooks on her desk. She comes from the nineteenth century, I think, because she certainly doesn't live in this one, and her only interests seem to be in the days of the early Romans and Greeks. They are very real to her, and she manages to make them pretty real to her students, most of the time. She *is* a bit weird, with her plain, dark skirts and white blouses, never varying, spring or fall, and her rather straggly gray hair pinned on top of her head with a big silver barrette.

I could see that Dennis found Miss Yancey's class really interesting, for he turned toward her almost eagerly, and he was right there with the correct answer when she called on him. I think that's what attracted me to him. I'd always noticed the intent way in which he listened to Miss Yancey's lectures, and I'd seen him with his friends: hazel eyes fixed on their faces, a ready smile or nod, as though he understood and agreed with whatever they were saying. No wonder he was popular. I hoped a little would rub off on me, because I'm not naturally outgoing. I always worry about what people think of me, instead of being relaxed and friendly with them.

Dennis was ahead of me when we left the room, and I watched him saunter down the hall: tall enough to tower over most of the other students, lean and muscular looking, a Christopher Reeve. Could I keep up with someone as sophisticated as he was? I felt as though I'd been in a little cocoon most of my life.

After school I went home, did a few chores around the house, and practiced my violin for a while. It came easier today, but for some reason my music didn't have the free flow it had had on Wednesday, when I'd come home from school, feeling so high because Dennis had asked me out. I guess I'd been living in a daydream that day and had had sober second thoughts since then.

"What are you going to wear tonight?" Mother asked, while I helped her with the meat loaf and scalloped potatoes for the family dinner.

"My blue cotton with the long sleeves, I think. The weather's still pretty warm, but it'll probably get cool later. I'll take my white sweater."

She nodded. "That looks nice with the blue. You'd better go get ready, Elizabeth. I'll finish up here. What time are you supposed to be there for dinner?"

"About six. Mrs. Boland usually doesn't get home from school too early, so they never eat before six." Actually, Amy did most of the dinner preparations because her mother's teaching job was in one of the small towns just outside our city, and Amy got home earlier.

"I put some ripe tomatoes in a plastic bag on the counter. Please take them to Mrs. Boland with my compliments. There are some paperback mysteries on the dining room table. Take them along, too, will you?"

I ran up to my room to dress. The blue cotton was pretty. After I was all dressed, I twirled in front of the mirror, feeling that I'd come out pretty well. The pale yellow hair, which Justin hated on himself, was undeniably an asset to me, and the blue dress, which I'd bought with my baby-sitting money, was cut well. It "gave me a figure" as Aunt Carolyn would say and made me look more sophisticated than I do in my normal outfit of jeans and blouse or sweater. I picked up my tote bag and sweater and ran down the stairs.

Amy's house is within walking distance, and I got there about fifteen minutes later, in time to mix the salad, to which I added three of the ripe tomatoes from our backyard garden. The house was quiet and neat as a pin. Amy is an only child, and Mrs. Boland doesn't believe in having pets because she works outside the home and animals are a lot of work. The house is an older one, completely remodeled, with all sorts of modern appliances, but lots of mellow old woodwork and window seats in the living room and in Amy's bedroom. I always feel happy there; it suits my nature, I guess. I especially love the little powder room, with its old-fashioned coat tree to hold big, fat towels, and its Victorian wallpaper and white wicker chairs.

"Cold beef, salad, and dessert tonight," Amy

said, filling the tea glasses and adding ice from a plastic bowl. "Not too fancy, but the dessert's apple pie Mom made last night."

"Sounds great."

Contentedly we went about our small jobs. Amy and I eat at each other's houses at least once a week, so it's all very comfortable and familiar.

Mrs. Boland came rushing in when things were almost ready. "Hi, girls! Sorry I'm so late. I had a meeting after school."

She and Amy are so much alike that you can see what Amy will look like when she's older. I've known Mrs. Boland since I was four years old, when the Bolands lived on our street, and I admire her a lot. She's bright and organized and has practical goals.

Mr. Boland came in a few minutes later, tousled my hair and Amy's, and sank back into a chair to enjoy the martini Mrs. Boland had mixed for him. He's a really nice man, not too tall, but sturdy looking, and he always has a little twinkle in his eyes. I've always considered the Bolands an ideal family.

We ate the cold sliced beef and the salad and hot, buttered french bread, and finally the apple pie with ice cream, but I was too nervous to enjoy it much. I kept thinking of Dennis and how wonderful he was. It seemed too good to be true, that we were dating. Tonight only, I reminded myself. Don't get your hopes up too high, girl.

"Come on," Amy said, after we'd stacked the dishes in the dishwasher and straightened up the kitchen for Mrs. Boland. "We can go comb our hair and listen to an album, until the boys come."

We went up to Amy's room, which looks like a bedroom from a magazine: simple, modern furniture with built-in bookcases and a desk, which I've always kind of coveted for my mother, it's so sleek and handsome and efficient. She put on an REO Speedwagon album, and we listened to that and tried out some new makeup Amy had gotten for her birthday. With lip gloss and eye makeup and a little subtle color on my cheekbones, I no longer looked like a feminine version of Justin. I looked pretty sophisticated, I thought. Even my natural blond hair looked satisfyingly artificial, like hair lightened at a good beauty shop.

Amy put on some makeup and ran a comb through her dark curly hair. I envied her. She and Kevin Murphy had been going steady for nearly two years now, and she was really comfortable with him. I thought how nice it must be to have a boyfriend you could depend on, one who would take you to parties and do homework with you and just be there when it was time to go skiing or dancing or to a rock concert or a movie. I won't say Amy was wildly in love with Kevin, but she liked him a lot, and they got along real well.

Until last year, I hadn't especially wanted a steady boyfriend. I was too caught up with my family and my violin and my schoolwork. But the last several months, I'd begun to wonder if I'd ever find someone who liked me enough to spend his weekends with me. I had gone out a few times and had double-dated with Amy and Kevin several times, but the guys I liked didn't especially like me, and for some reason, I never seemed to like the boys who were attracted to me. Until Dennis Whitcomb sat down opposite me in the library.

The front doorbell rang, and Amy said, "There they are!" She gave one last look in the mirror, picked up her jacket, and said, "Come on, let's go meet your fate!"

Amy ran down the stairs, and I followed more sedately, trying not to look too eager. And there they were, standing in the entry hall, looking absolutely marvelous, both of them! Kevin is kind of short and dark-haired and smiling, like Amy, and Dennis, in designer jeans and a matching blue sweater, looked terrific. I could feel my hands grow clammy, and I rubbed them surreptitiously on the sides of my blue dress but then began to worry in case I'd streaked it. Some sophisticate, wiping my hands on my clean dress, like my grubby little sister or brother.

"Hi, Elizabeth," Dennis said. "You look great."

"Thanks." I stopped myself just in time from saying, "So do you." Women's lib or not, you just don't say things like that to a boy you hardly know, so I smiled at him idiotically and tried to think of something sparkling to say.

Fortunately the conversation quickly became general and silly and lots of fun. Amy has a great sense of humor, and so does Kevin, and they started things rolling, but Dennis was not exactly quiet. Before I knew it, I was talking, too, as though I'd known Dennis as long as I had Kevin and Amy.

The Woody Allen movie wasn't one of his best, but we laughed a lot anyway.

Dennis casually reached over and took my hand during the movie. It seemed so natural— and so wonderful. His fingers were warm and strong, and I could feel the pulse leaping from his wrist to mine, or so it seemed. For that hour and a half, we were linked together, the way you are with your best friend when you're a little kid and you prick your fingers and rub them together and swear to be blood brothers forever. I had had my hand held before, but I'd never felt so warm and loving and cared-for.

After the movie Kevin said, "Hey, how would you all like to go to that country-and-western place over on the north side?" Then he grinned at me. "I know that's not your type of music, Lizzie, but how about trying it for a change?"

I could feel my face flushing. "I like all kinds of music. Ask Amy if I'm not a real rock fan."

"What does he mean?" Dennis asked, curious.

Amy said, in a staunch way, "She plays the violin *beautifully*. Mostly classical stuff. But sure, she likes rock, too. Who doesn't?"

Dennis was looking at me as though he were seeing me for the first time. "Why didn't you tell me this before? And how come you're not playing in the school orchestra?" He gave a kind of sheepish grin. "I play the clarinet because my mother thought I should play *some* instrument, and that's the only one I could master."

Kevin gave a great hoot of laughter. "That's not the right word for the way you play the clarinet, Den!"

Dennis feinted a poke at Kevin's chin, but he admitted, "It's true, I don't play very well, just loud. They took me in the orchestra because they needed another woodwind."

We were crossing the half-deserted parking lot to Kevin's car, and Dennis caught my hand in his again. "I'm serious, girl. Why haven't you tried out for the orchestra? We need you!"

I shook my head. "I don't know. I just don't play in public. I practice at home a lot, and I play for my relatives and sometimes my friends, but that's all."

"You're shy."

"I'm not!" How could I explain to him that the violin was the hidden part of me, the part I couldn't show the world? I had no intention of making it my career, although I had thought of becoming a high-school music teacher. But the making of music, that gift from my father, was both secret and sacred. I had no desire to stand up in front of other students and try out for the school orchestra.

We got in the backseat of Kevin's car, and over the roar of the motor, Dennis said, "I want to hear you play. I like people who do things well."

"Ha! I might be a rotten musician, for all you know!"

He shook his head. "Not you. I can tell. Besides, Amy vouches for you."

Then we were off to the Cowpoke, a country-and-western place where I'd never been. It was patronized mostly by teenagers, for it didn't have a bar. It had a charge to get in, and I'd heard the soft drinks were pretty expensive, but it was a place where we didn't need ID cards.

The Cowpoke was on the river; it was an old flour mill that had been converted into an old-time dance hall. I liked it right away because everything was authentic: the mismatched wooden chairs and oak tables, the beams towering above our heads, the faded posters dating from the 1890s. On a wooden platform, a little four-piece band was playing country-and-western music. Not only the members of the band but many of the customers wore ten-gallon hats and elaborate cowboy boots—in New York State, no less!

Music is music, and even though I wasn't used to it, I liked the country stuff right away. We got up to dance, and I thought I was in heaven, dancing with Dennis Whitcomb. His smooth style made my own dancing better than it normally was. After they had played a couple of fast songs, the band went into one of those long, sad ballads about a truck driver who came home and found his wife with another man and how he wanted to shoot them but instead got into his big old truck and headed, "Hell Bent for Election," as the song said.

"Life is pretty dramatic for these guys," Dennis said, pitching his voice above the music. "Makes things around here sound pretty boring, doesn't it?"

I nodded. "If you listen to the words, it sounds terribly sad, but the music is so upbeat, it's hard to believe the words."

Finally the boys went up to the polished wooden bar, which now served as a counter, and got a large pizza loaded with pepperoni, mushrooms, green peppers, and cheese.

"It's enormous!" I said. "We'll never eat it all."

"Wanna bet?" said Dennis.

We did eat it, of course, washing it down with cola and ginger ale. The boys ate most of it, but Amy and I weren't exactly dainty. I don't know just when the talk became serious. Both Kevin

42

and Dennis were seniors, and they were excited about college the next year.

"I'm not really sure what I want to be," Kevin admitted. "Not a CPA like my father. He seems to like it, but I think it's the pits, the same old stuff day after day. I may go into computer engineering. It's a big field, and you get to work in foreign countries, if you want to."

Dennis's eyes glowed. "I've known since I was six years old what I want to be—a doctor. A pediatrician. It seems to me that keeping kids healthy and making the sick ones well is a really worthwhile thing to do."

He grinned at me. "I'm a one-track person, and I plan to forge ahead till I get that shingle, as my mother calls it. No offense, Elizabeth, but that's why I date a lot of girls. It's not that I'm that fickle, just practical. I don't want to be sidetracked."

My heart fell with a thud. I knew that he was trying to tell me something. An idiot would have known that. He really meant that he didn't plan to get serious about any one girl. And here I'd been hoping that somehow, some way, Dennis Whitcomb would be consumed by love of Elizabeth Ashton, girl dimwit.

I said primly, "I think that's a really worthwhile goal, and I know you'll make it. And they say high-school students have no purpose in life except to drink and take drugs and party!"

He laughed, and I knew he was relieved that

I'd taken it so lightly. At least that's what *he* thought. I got up to dance with him again, but the joy had gone out of the evening. Laughing and joking, I acted as though I were having the time of my life that night, but it was all acting. I was surprised at the good show I could put on when I wanted to.

Finally we were all tired, and the music seemed extra loud, and we decided it was time to go home. My mother hadn't set a curfew, but I knew she'd be expecting me home soon, so I was relieved when Kevin suggested leaving.

"I have to be at work at nine tomorrow," Kevin said. He worked at a gas station and was paying for his car with the money he earned.

Dennis said, "I don't have to be at work till ten." To me he added, "My uncle is a doctor, and I work in his office on Saturdays, partly for pay but mostly for the experience."

Since both Amy and I had just turned sixteen, our jobs had been limited mostly to babysitting. We could stay in bed all morning if we wanted to . . . theoretically, that is. Mrs. Boland usually pressed Amy into service cleaning house, and Bonita and Justin were so noisy on Saturdays that no one could possibly sleep very late.

We all piled into Kevin's car again, Dennis and I in the backseat. Amy had asked me if I wanted to stay all night at her house, but I'd decided I wouldn't carry things quite that far. Dennis might as well see which part of town I lived in, and it would be too late for them to come in, so that was all right.

We were all a little quieter now, tired from the long evening and the food and the loud music and the dancing. Dennis sat really close to me and pulled my head over onto his shoulder. It was heaven. I wanted that ride to go on forever, instead of just the twenty minutes it took to get to my street. All the time we were riding, he held my hand in his warm, strong one. We hardly said anything to each other, but there was the most wonderful feeling of empathy, of not *having* to say anything. I put out of my mind all that he'd said about being single-minded, of not having a special girl, because he had to get his education first. For these few minutes, it didn't matter. I was enjoying the moment and not worrying about tomorrow.

Finally we pulled up in front of my little house. There was a light burning in the living room and one in my mother's workroom. She doesn't go to bed when I'm out for the evening, not even when I baby-sit.

"I'll go on in," I said quickly. "My mother's waiting up for me."

"Whatever you say," Dennis murmured. He leaned over and kissed me, so gently and tenderly that my bones seemed to turn to water. "I'll call you," he said, "and I'll see you at school. Thanks for a wonderful evening, Elizabeth."

Somehow I wrenched open the door and got

out of the car on my shaky legs. Somehow I said good night to everyone and ran up the walk to my front door. I heard the shouts of my friends and heard the car pull away as I let myself in the house. I hoped Mother was too engrossed in her work to come and greet me, hoped everyone else was sound asleep, for I wanted to run, no, to *leap*, up the stairs to my room and think about that kiss. No matter how Dennis might feel about me, I knew, without a doubt, that I was in love for the first time in my life.

Chapter Five

Sunday was a great day. In the afternoon I helped Mother bake cookies for Bonita's class picnic the next day. I cut Michelle's hair and helped Justin with his homework. I was so happy that I wanted everyone else to be happy.

"I'll help you with the tomatoes," I said eagerly to my mother. Our plants had yielded several bushels of fat, red tomatoes, and Mother had decided they must be canned.

"They'll be wonderful in the dead of winter," she had said. "I'll make chili with them. There's nothing like home-canned tomatoes to give flavor to chili."

She had already sterilized the fruit jars, and I helped her plunge the crimson tomatoes into hot water so that we could slide the thin skins off. Then we stuffed them into the sparkling clean jars, added salt, and put them in the canner on the back of the stove. The aroma was

47

wonderful, spicy, pungent—a smell of September. I had smelled it all my life: the aroma of tomatoes and chili sauce, things that smell even better than they taste, like coffee.

Michelle, tall and slender and elegant, even at twelve, wandered into the kitchen, poured herself a glass of lemonade, and sat on the stepstool, watching us lazily.

"You could help," I said, but it was impossible to quarrel with her today. I felt too happy.

She could see that I wasn't about to pursue the subject, so she only raised an eyebrow at me and sipped the lemonade. "When I'm a well-known lawyer," she said superciliously, "I'm never going to have a garden, and I'm never going to can anything. I plan to live on frozen fruits and vegetables, plus steak and lobster and caviar."

Mother adjusted the flame under the canner and then came and collapsed in a chair. "You've never tasted caviar in your life," she said, "and, as I recall, you didn't even like lobster when we had it at the Lobster Pot last year."

Michelle was unflappable. "Well, you know what I mean. I plan to live high and not worry about how much things cost. I'll probably have a cook."

Mother said dryly, "You have a cook now—me. Now kindly get up off your seat and get a glass of lemonade for Elizabeth and me. Then you can wash up the pots and pans."

We took our lemonade out onto the back steps and sat there contentedly. Mother glanced at me sideways. "I take it you had a good time Friday night."

I could feel the smile tugging at my mouth. "You guessed it. I had a great time. Did I tell you what we did?" I gave her a quick rundown of Friday night's activities, just in case she'd missed anything.

"I take it Dennis proved to be as wonderful as you expected him to be."

"Oh, yes! And he said he'd call me. I think he really meant it."

"Of course he meant it, silly. Why wouldn't he?" My mother is unrealistic, but there's something very reassuring about her optimism and her genuine belief in our capabilities and our wonderful qualities. It's nice to know that at least one person in the world thinks you're great.

I tried to explain. "It's like—Dennis has this whole life that's totally different, totally apart from mine. The only real connecting link between us is that we go to the same school, and he's kind of friendly with Kevin. If we hadn't met casually in Miss Yancey's history class and then run into each other in the school library, we might never have really met at all, because he's a year ahead of me. Don't you see?

"Both of his parents are attorneys, and they're always being written up in the paper for being on special boards and things." I laughed, but I meant it. "I suppose they're what you'd call civic leaders."

"And that makes Dennis different from your other friends?"

I was petting Figaro absently. "Yes, it really does, Mother. All my other friends are regular people, but Dennis's family is set apart." I hesitated, searching for words. "Not because they have money but because they're the kind of people who *do* things. It's not just social activity, it's civic activity, I guess."

She nodded. "I can understand your thinking, Elizabeth, and in a way, you may be right. But I don't want you to be humble with Dennis. You have your own strengths, your own gifts, and they're just as important as his. After all, he hasn't had time to prove himself, has he? And he can't lay claim to his parents' achievements."

How could I explain to her the power and drive I felt coming from Dennis? "He's good at whatever he does, Mother. He's a basketball star, and he works on the school paper, and he's an A student, and he plays in the school orchestra. And that's just part of the list!" Then I added, "He wants me to try out for the orchestra. Amy told him I play the violin."

She gave me an emphatic nod. "Good for him. Perhaps he'll have more success with you than I've had."

I shook my head. "I doubt it."

Just then the phone rang, and I sprang to my feet. It could be Dennis! Slamming the screen door, I dashed into the kitchen, where Michelle, an expression of distaste on her face, was cleaning the pots and pans. "You couldn't answer that, could you?" I flung at her as I ran to the hallway.

Snatching up the telephone, I uttered a breathless, "Hello?"

It was Dennis! "Hi," he said, "how are things going?"

"Fine," I said, "just fine. How about you?"

"I have to go out to Lesterville with my parents," he said. "But I thought I'd call and check on you first. What're you doing?"

Lesterville is at Lake Canoga and is one of *the* elite places to have a summer cottage. It's one of those places they advertise on TV, with sand and a sailboat and Beautiful People lying around looking beautiful and staring at their expensive condominiums.

I forced myself to answer him. "I've been helping my mother can tomatoes." Did anything ever sound more mundane?

There was a little silence, and then he said, "I don't think I ever saw anyone do that." He laughed. "I suppose I thought they came all ready in those shiny tin cans."

I tried to be flip. "Shows you haven't been around. All us backyard farmers preserve tomatoes about this time of year."

His voice sounded almost wistful. "I wish I were there watching you, instead of having to hang around the beach with people I don't particularly care about."

I could actually feel my pulse leap. Did he mean that I was a person he did care about? "I wish you were, too," I said, trying to sound completely casual.

We talked for a few minutes, and then he said, "I hear my father calling, so I suppose I'd better get going. I'll call you tomorrow night, OK?"

The next second the phone was humming in my hand. I sat there cradling it as though it were alive. He'd said he'd call me tomorrow! It was something so wonderful to look forward to that I felt like flying. The only way I could express my euphoria was to play the violin, of course, and I ran upstairs to do just that.

When I walked into the lunchroom the next day, I looked around quickly, hoping to see Dennis, hoping he'd be looking for me. Amy and Kevin and Bob Thrasher were waving at me, and I got my tray and went toward their table. But I had glimpsed Dennis. This time he was sitting at a table way over in the corner, and there was just one person sitting with him— Melissa Cooper.

Amy looked critically at my tray. "It's scalloped corn and hamburgers today, and you love them. How come you've just got a little dish of cottage cheese and Jell-O?"

"I'm dieting," I said. I couldn't explain that the lump in my throat would make it difficult to eat anything.

Bob looked at me in a very flattering way. "You're just right, Liz. Don't take off an ounce."

I sighed. "I probably won't. It's easier to put on a pound than to take off an ounce."

Bob is nice, very quiet, and a little shy. He's going to be a research scientist, and I sometimes think he doesn't find the outside world too interesting. He'd rather be looking at cells under a microscope than at live people. I had gone out with him a few times, but we remained just friends.

Trying not to let my gaze wander over into that far corner, I talked to my friends and pretended to eat my lunch. Of all the people who could have been sitting with Dennis, Melissa Cooper was the one I hated most to have there. She was senior class president and sure to be prom queen. She was a beautiful, positive, snobby girl who had never spoken directly to me, even though she was in my French class. I knew that she was the sort of girl Dennis deserved—and probably wanted. I hated her.

I picked at the cottage cheese, then let the strawberry Jell-O slide down my throat, and all the time I laughed and joked with my friends, as though I hadn't a care in the world. Women are great actresses, I think.

I was so engrossed in my playacting that I didn't see them leave the corner table, so I jumped when a hand touched my shoulder, and a voice said, "Hi, Elizabeth."

I turned around, and there was Dennis. A little to one side, as though she wanted to remain aloof, was Melissa Cooper. I thought for a second how much she looked like Brooke Shields, and my heart sank. He must be showing me, showing all of us, that Melissa was his special girl.

Dennis turned to her and said, "Do you know Elizabeth Ashton and Amy Boland and Kevin Murphy?" He looked inquiringly at Bob, who swallowed a huge bite of hamburger before he said, "Bob Thrasher."

Melissa gave a sort of sweeping, "Hi," to all of us juniors, as though she'd never seen us before in her life. And Parkleigh High School isn't that huge. I don't know about the rest of them, but she made me feel like a nothing.

"Wednesday afternoon they're having tryouts for the orchestra," Dennis said to me. "Promise you'll come—and bring your violin!"

Did I imagine a tiny twinge of envy on Melissa's perfect face? Perhaps that look was what made me bold enough to say, "I might. I'm not sure. I told you I don't play in public."

Melissa lifted an eyebrow. "Does that mean

you're a professional? Why haven't we heard about you?"

Amy said loyally, "She's good enough to be a professional, but she's too darned modest. Let's all push her along."

Dennis's hand was on my shoulder. "Right. We're all pushing, Elizabeth. Wednesday. Promise?"

I couldn't believe the words coming out of my mouth. "OK, I promise. If only I don't chicken out by then!"

"You won't chicken out," Dennis said, his voice stern. "I'll see you there." He gave my shoulder a little squeeze, then followed Melissa out of the lunchroom.

All afternoon long, the memory of that warm, strong hand on my shoulder remained with me. It even blocked out—almost—the memory of Melissa Cooper's pretty, sophisticated face.

Chapter Six

After school Amy and I walked home together. We talked mostly about Dennis—after all, we'd talked about Kevin plenty of times in the past. It really felt good to talk about a boy I liked. It was sort of like becoming part of the human race. Nothing seemed quite as important as love.

"Do you think he really likes me?" I asked, for about the tenth time.

Amy's opinions are always very firm. "Of course he does. I could tell the other night. And look how he came over to you today, to make sure you were going to try out for the orchestra."

My tone became a little glum then. "Yeah, but look who he had with him. Miss America of Parkleigh High."

"Doesn't matter. They've been friends for years. Someone told me that. If there'd been anything between them, he wouldn't have stopped to talk to you."

I could have listened to her reassuring words for hours, but she had chores to do at home, and so did I, so we parted company. I sauntered along, dreaming dreams, putting myself at the very center of parties at Dennis's home, placing myself in his arms in some romantic, wooded spot, dancing with him at the country club. With imagination, I could be the most glamorous girl in the whole school, the most beautiful, the most enchanting. And now I really had someone to dream about.

When I entered the house through the kitchen door, I could feel something brewing. It leaked out of the walls and bounced off the ceilings. I could hear Bonita's high, sweet voice and Michelle's cool one, both sounding excited. I went looking for them.

They were all in Mother's study, even Justin, who is usually outdoors, no matter what the weather. "What's going on?" I asked.

They were all grinning. Justin couldn't wait. "Mother sold a story!" he said.

"Oh, that's great!" I said and threw my arms around Mother. "To whom?"

"To *Secret Stories*, and for a nice round sum." She waved the check at me. "Payment on acceptance instead of on publication. How do you like them apples?"

Bonita said, "It's just like Christmas! Mother said we can go out to dinner Saturday night, and we can each have something special—a present, I mean." On impulse I ran upstairs and got my violin and brought it back to the study. I couldn't think of a piece entirely suitable to the occasion, so I began to play some Strauss waltzes because they sound so festive. Pretty soon everyone was whirling around the room, pretending to dance, although no one really knew how to waltz, not even Mother.

Then I heard the phone ringing, and I stopped the music and went to answer it. It was Dennis.

"What's up?" he asked. "I can hear voices in the background."

"My mother sold a short story. We're celebrating."

"Wow! That's wonderful! I never knew a writer before." He laughed. "Well, actually the daughter of a writer, but it comes down to the same thing, doesn't it? What a talented family you have. Are the younger kids into writing books or leading symphonies or anything?"

I laughed. "Not yet, but they probably will be in a couple of years. I think Justin was born about thirty-five years old." I had told him about my younger sisters and my little brother, and he had seemed fascinated.

"When you're the only one, a big family is so interesting, like part of another world," he'd said.

Now he told me, "I'm a great reader—my whole

family is—so I guess I have special feelings of admiration for people like your mother. How does she do it—turn thoughts into stories?"

"Well, it's just a story for a confession magazine," I said modestly.

"Doesn't matter. It's something she created out of nothing."

"That's true. She can take a tiny news item from the paper and work it into a story about a young woman with a real problem. It is wonderful, when I think about it."

We talked for a little longer, mostly about school and things, but all the time I was mentally hugging myself because he'd called me. At this moment, I hardly cared that he had had lunch with Melissa Cooper and that he didn't want to be serious about any one girl. I was simply happy because he'd called me and because we could talk together so freely and openly.

Finally he said, "I'd better let you go and celebrate with your family. Now don't forget to take your violin with you Wednesday. I expect to see you in the auditorium that afternoon, auditioning for the orchestra."

"If I can work myself up to it," I said.

"You'd better." His voice was firm and just faintly bossy, but I liked it.

Prentice and Figaro and the other cats were in the kitchen when I went out there. Recklessly I gave them all some raw hamburger, because it seemed only fair that they celebrate, too. They were part of the family, and they seemed to sense excitement in the house.

I went back to the study then and hugged Mother again and told her what Dennis had said. She seemed very pleased.

Bonita said, "Mother said we can go out for hamburgers tonight, even if it *isn't* anybody's birthday."

"No cooking and no dishes tonight," Mother said triumphantly.

We're probably the last living Americans not to own a car, so we all trooped on foot to the nearest McDonald's, which fortunately is only three blocks from our house. Mother, Michelle, and I went to the counter and got the trays of hamburgers, french fries, and milk shakes. "The works," Mother had said firmly, although normally she doesn't believe in having several carbohydrates at one meal.

Maybe it's true that you appreciate things more if you don't have too many of them, for we all ate those burgers as though they were expensive steaks. Bonita and Justin had little milk shake mustaches above their lips, and even blasé Michelle relaxed and enjoyed herself.

"This really is fun," Michelle said. "Thanks, Mother. And promise you'll get something special for yourself."

"I will. New shoes, probably, and a blouse or

two for winter." She looked around at her family. "Have you all decided what you'd like for a special gift?"

"Not clothes," Justin said firmly.

Mother laughed. "In addition to some school clothes."

Bonita said, "A tiny radio, all for me, like Tracy's." Tracy was her best friend and sometimes her rival.

Michelle ate two more french fries before she said, "Pierced ears and little gold hoops for my ears."

Mother looked a little sad. "I guess you're growing up, Michelle. I'd thought I wouldn't have this particular argument with you for another year or two." She sighed. "I did promise what you wanted most, and if pierced ears are it, then you'll have them."

Justin drank the last of his milk shake and announced, "Books. I'd like a book on frogs, and if that doesn't cost too much, a book on ancient Romans."

No use asking Justin why he's reading about any particular subject. He's a born student and is always reading up on something.

"Elizabeth?" Mother looked at me. "What would you like?"

I shook my head. "I can't think of anything right now. I really don't need anything." Then I saw her face, vulnerable for just a moment, and

I added quickly, "But if you're really bent on wasting your money on me, I wouldn't mind the new Itzhak Perlman album. He's so wonderful."

The happiness came back to her face, and the conversation became general, but I was silent, thinking of how I could have hurt my mother by refusing her gift. Her love for us was almost a tangible thing, something beautiful and constant in an ever-changing world. I knew she would give us everything, if she could.

On the way home, Mother and I fell behind the others. I told her more about Dennis's phone call and that he admired her for being a writer. "He thinks we're a talented family," I said. "He wanted me to promise to take my violin to school Wednesday and try out for the orchestra."

"And will you do it?"

"I can't make up my mind." Then I added honestly, "I'm so scared, Mother. Mr. Greeley is famous for being a perfectionist, and he's hard on the kids in the orchestra. And don't forget, all the other members of the orchestra will be sitting there, listening to me, judging me."

Mother was quiet for a minute. "Elizabeth, Uncle Bob thinks you're good, and I think you're good, but the important thing is for *you* to think you're good. I think you should have enough confidence in your ability to try out for the school orchestra. But even if you don't make it—and I think that's a very remote possibility— you'll have tried. The important thing is to have a dream."

I took a deep breath. "OK," I said, "I'll try!"

Chapter Seven

On Wednesday morning, I put a couple of pieces of sheet music in my violin case and set off for school. I was shaking inside because I really was terrified of the audition. This is silly, I kept telling myself, you've played for relatives and friends of the family. Mr. Greeley can't be any worse than Aunt Carolyn, and the orchestra members are your classmates, for heaven's sake. But deep down, I knew it was Dennis Whitcomb who bothered me. Amy had given me such a glowing testimonial that I was afraid I couldn't live up to it. And I needed to excel in one thing, I thought, in order to keep Dennis interested in me.

At lunchtime he stopped at our table and said sternly, "Did you bring your violin?"

I nodded. "Yes, but I'm still scared. Mr. Greeley is a real musician, you know, and I don't think he's too fascinated by amateurs."

Dennis laughed. "He took me, didn't he? I must be the rankest amateur in that whole orchestra. Come on, Elizabeth. Amy says you're good. Now be there."

I said weakly, "I'll be there."

He went out, and Melissa Cooper, Bat Saunders, and Suzie Hall trailed behind him. Dennis Whitcomb never seemed to lack friends. And despite Amy's assurance that Melissa and Dennis were old friends, I couldn't help feeling jealous of her. Her air toward Dennis was definitely not platonic, although his attitude toward her seemed casual enough. Perhaps this was all part of playing the field, though. He'd said he didn't plan to get involved with any one girl until he finished medical school, and the best way to avoid involvement was to have more than one girlfriend.

At three o'clock I went rushing down the hallway with several hundred other students, trying to get to my locker quickly. Parkleigh High is an older school, a two-story brick building with long corridors and faintly musty-smelling classrooms and lots of shiny brown linoleum. The lockers are dark green and smell like gym suits. The place has a lot of character, and I don't really mind that it's not a sprawling suburban high school with lots of sunlight and study "areas."

I took out my violin case and went hurrying off to the auditorium, where the orchestra held rehearsals. I was a little late, and everyone was already assembled on the stage. It looked like the New York Philharmonic to me—dozens and dozens of faces. They all looked professional somehow, very serious, with their instruments resting in their laps or standing up beside them—depending upon the sizes, of course. I picked out Dennis and his clarinet and Amy and her trumpet and a few other people I knew, but mostly they seemed like cool, appraising strangers, ready to judge me and my talent.

Mr. Greeley strode down the aisle toward the stage. He is tall and very thin and has a shock of wavy, black hair and a mustache like that of an old-time cowboy. He's a graduate of Juilliard, a strict conductor, and he's been known to throw people out of the orchestra just for playing a few wrong notes during a concert. Playing for him would be nothing like playing for Uncle Bob, who is gentle and encouraging.

Unfortunately, I was the only one auditioning that day. It would have been easier if a few real amateurs had been trying out, but it was just me.

"Elizabeth Ashton," he said, in a loud voice. He was standing near me by then, and I jumped a foot.

"Here," I said, my voice barely coming out.

"Your counselor has given me your name. She said you'd like to audition. Did you bring your music?"

"Yes." Fumbling, I took out the sheet music.

Mr. Greeley looked sideways at my music. "And?" he said.

"I thought—I thought I'd try 'Hora Staccato.' "

He raised his thick, triangular eyebrows. "That's very ambitious for one so young. But go ahead."

I stood up by my seat, but he motioned me to a more open spot, just below the stage apron. I could feel everyone looking down on me, but most of all I was conscious of Mr. Greeley's appraising eye.

"Someone hand me a music stand," he said, and Dennis dashed over and lowered his stand into Mr. Greeley's waiting grasp. Dennis gave me a wink, and I smiled weakly. Even that wide, infectious smile did little for me today. I was too scared.

I loved the Danicu piece, a difficult one, a challenge to me and to all violinists, I guess, but the opening bars came out wavering and faintly squeaky, and I heard someone give a tiny snicker. It was such a spirited piece, but there was no spirit in my rendering of it. I could feel the tears welling up, and I was ready to lay down my bow and call it quits. Then I looked up and saw Amy smiling at me, saw her put thumb and forefinger together in a little round O, saw Dennis's encouraging smile, and I stopped playing.

"I'm sorry," I said to Mr. Greeley, "I'm nervous, and I got off to a bad start. May I try again?"

He held out both palms in a gesture that indicated I could start again; I straightened my shoulders and began playing again. This time it was all right, this time the violin sang, and the bow flew over the strings like silk, like water over smooth stones. I forgot all of them, even Dennis, forgot everything but the music and the wonderful instrument, which seemed to have become part of me.

When I'd finished, there was a little silence, and my heart sank. Had the beauty been only in my own mind? But a moment later, there was applause, spontaneous, wonderful applause from my peers, and I could feel my cheeks turning pink.

Mr. Greeley was actually smiling. Once again he spread out his hands. "Well, Elizabeth Ashton," he said, "I guess you're the newest member of the orchestra."

Standing there with my violin clutched in my arms, I had the most wonderful sense of joy, and I knew, perhaps for the first time in my life, what it meant to achieve something completely on my own. Well, not completely, of course. The talent was a gift, the glorious music was a gift from the composer, but my hard work had brought them together and given them life and beauty. I felt as my mother must feel when she has finished and sold a story, when she has brought characters to life and given them meaning.

I went up the creaky wooden steps and sat on the stage, as Mr. Greeley told me to do. People were smiling at me, and both Dennis and Amy gave little waves of welcome. Now that it was all over, I wondered why I'd been so terrified—and why I hadn't done it long before.

Then began all that lovely scraping and tooting and shuffling of feet that an orchestra does before a concert. This was only a rehearsal, of course, but the sound was the same, and it was tremendously exciting to someone like me. Until now, I'd played strictly on my own, since no one else in the family, except my father and Uncle Bob, was musical.

After the rehearsal, Dennis came over to me. "What did I tell you!" he said. "I just knew you'd make it—and I also knew you were really talented."

"How could you know?" I asked. "You'd never heard me play until today."

"I did know, though." He swung my hands in his. "Come on, let's go over to McGillicutty's and have a milk shake or hamburger or something to celebrate your victory. Do you have time?"

"Sure."

We went out into the rain, but it didn't matter to me. It was a glorious day because Dennis's strong arm was around my shoulders and

he was hurrying me across the street to McGillicutty's. I had my violin case under one arm, and
it kept slipping, and in three seconds the rain
had plastered my hair in my eyes, but I couldn't
have been happier.

The sweet aroma of fresh-baked cookies and
the mouth-watering smell of really good hamburgers filled the air of Parkleigh High's favorite lunch place. Few adults ate there, probably
because the din of teenage voices would have
been too much for them. The food was good
and pretty reasonable, and Mac and his wife
loved teenagers and tolerated an awful lot. I
guess they figured no one could harm the black-
and-white tile floor and the varnished wooden
booths too much.

"Dennis!" I could grow to hate that high-
pitched, slightly affected voice, I thought. It was
Melissa Cooper, waving from a corner booth,
where she was sitting with another girl and two
boys.

He waved casually but continued to guide me
toward a vacant booth at the opposite end of
the long, narrow room.

She wasn't used to being ignored. "Dennis, I
want to talk to you."

"Later, Melissa," he called. "We're starved."
He grinned at me. "I've known her since we
were two. She was spoiled then."

His words made me feel so lighthearted. If he
took this brotherly attitude toward Melissa, I

could conquer my jealousy of her. He pushed me to the inside of the booth and sat down beside me instead of taking the seat opposite me.

Immediately I was conscious of his body touching mine, his warm breath close to my cheek, his hand on mine. I laughed nervously and, with my other hand, brushed the wet strands of hair back from my forehead. "I must look terrible."

He frowned. "Why are you always putting yourself down, Elizabeth? You look very pretty, and you ought to know that. And you pretended you weren't especially good at the violin, and you were wonderful. Why don't you have more faith in yourself?"

I didn't know what to say. Was I always putting myself down? I envied the easy confidence of Melissa Cooper or of Dennis himself, but their lives had been pretty different from mine. Having your father die sort of pulls the rug out from under you.

My easy, happy mood had dissipated, but I tried to smile at him. "My mother gave me that lecture yesterday. I guess it must be true. I'll try to be more aggressive from now on!"

"Well, maybe not aggressive. Confident would be better, Elizabeth."

"OK, confident," I said, and I smiled at him confidently.

We ordered from one of the college-girl waitresses—hamburger and fries and Coke for Dennis, chocolate milk shake for me—and sat talking so comfortably that I felt as though I'd known him forever. People stopped by, some of them school leaders with whom I'd had only limited contact before, and some of my friends waved at us. I couldn't help feeling proud. This was the way life should be, sitting beside a boy you liked, surrounded by friends and acquaintances, being part of the school social scene.

'But most of all, I liked the fact that Dennis was so open about this date with me. He might not plan on having a special girl, but by bringing me to the place where practically the whole school hung out and by being so attentive in front of everybody, he certainly made me feel special.

As for me, I had never felt even remotely like this about any boy. My experience was pretty limited, admittedly, but nothing had prepared me for this—this feeling of pure joy, this sonata of love.

Chapter Eight

All the next day it rained, but I hardly noticed. Nothing could mar my mood, not even Michelle returning my pink blouse with an unremovable chocolate stain on one cuff.

"That's OK," I told her graciously. "It doesn't show very much."

She looked at me in disbelief. "Are you sick or something?"

I thought of an expression I had once heard or read—I didn't remember where. "For I am sick with love." Whoever had said it had said something very descriptive, very true. I just smiled at her, like a person in some sort of happy delirium, and she went away shaking her head. We'd had a lot of fights in the past over clothes. We were built differently but could wear each other's blouses. I knew she had dreaded telling me about the stain because she had expected a burst of fury from me.

I hadn't even minded that Dennis had eaten lunch with some of his same old crowd, and that included girls. Obviously he wasn't going to change his habits just because of me, but as he left the lunchroom, he stopped to say hello and put his hand on my shoulder. That touch warmed me for the whole afternoon.

Amy and I walked home together that afternoon, since neither of us had after-school activities. "Let's hurry a little bit," she said as I dawdled. "It's raining, Lizbeth."

"I don't care," I told her dreamily. "I love the rain."

"You love everything right now," she said, "because you're in love with Dennis Whitcomb."

"I'm not!" I could feel the color surging to my cheeks in a way I hated. "I *like* him. It's too soon to say love."

She shrugged. "Call it what you want to. It looks like love to me."

With some dignity, I picked up my pace and marched along beside her. Actually, I knew there was some truth in what she said, but I decided to ignore it. We walked along, discussing one of the books on our required reading list in English. I'd been mulling something over in my mind, though.

"Amy, how would you like to try out for cheerleader? I think it might be fun to try, at least." I carefully made my tone noncommittal, hoping she wouldn't guess I wanted to be a cheerleader because Melissa Cooper was one.

She stopped and stared at me in astonishment. "What brought that on? I thought we'd agreed long ago that cheerleading is for exhibitionists. Besides, I'm not athletic enough. They'd never take me."

"I thought the orchestra would never take me, but they did. Maybe it's time to plunge into newer, greater things. I kind of like a challenge, Amy."

She wrinkled her nose. "I hate gym, and I'm certainly not going to seek it out and try out for cheerleader. I'm just not the type to stand out on a football field and jump up in the air and shout and wave a golden pom-pom. Count me out."

"OK, but I think I'll try out next week." Brave words, but actually I needed Amy for moral support. I couldn't quite picture myself doing something so extroverted without her there to cheer me on. We'd done things together for so long that I'd grown to count on her.

That evening, instead of practicing my violin very much, I stayed in my room and rehearsed some of the routines that I remembered the cheerleaders doing at games. As I practiced, I became excited at the thought that I might be chosen. Dennis wasn't on the football team, but lots of his friends were, and I was sure he attended all the games. I could picture myself, one of a line of girls, swaying and dancing in the October sunshine, waving the pom-poms, cheering our team on to victory.

I'd just finished a particularly high leap, when I heard someone beating on my door. It was Bonita, her delicate little face looking very severe. "Mother says to find out what you're doing and to ask you to be a little more quiet. She's writing, and Michelle and I are doing our homework." She glanced around my room. "Michelle said to check to see if you have a herd of elephants up here."

"OK, you fresh little kid," I said. "Go back and tell everyone I'll be quiet from now on."

The next day, a Friday, was bright and sunny, and I practiced out in the backyard, hoping the neighbors wouldn't see me and think I'd gone stark-raving mad. Fortunately Mother had gone out to lunch with a friend, and the others weren't home yet. Only Prentice noticed me, and he raced around the yard barking excitedly because he thought I was playing a new game. I thought I was getting pretty good—after all, I'd practiced secretly many times before, without ever expecting to have the courage to go to the tryouts.

It was all surface, however. Inside, deep down inside where the things that matter most are, I was thinking of Dennis. Would he call and ask me out this weekend, or had last Friday's date and our casual get-together at McGillicutty's been it? I couldn't let myself think that. I had to believe that he would call me sooner or later.

And so I moped away the weekend, listening for the phone, snapping at my sisters and brother, doing a little work around the house, fingering the violin listlessly, being nice to Aunt Carolyn and Uncle Bob when they dropped in for coffee.

I knew that Amy and Kevin were going out Saturday night, and I could hardly wait to hear from her Sunday morning. I thought, however, that she was a little reluctant to talk to me. "Where did you go, Amy?"

"A movie, the John Travolta one. It was good."

"And?"

"After that we went to Gitzy's Hamburger Joint to eat. It was kind of dead there, so we came home early and watched a movie on TV."

I couldn't help asking it. "Did you see Dennis anywhere?"

She hesitated, and I knew she didn't want to tell me, but Amy never lies. "Come on, Amy, I know I don't own him."

"He and Melissa were at Gitzy's. They stopped at our booth and talked for a few minutes."

My heart sank, but I said lightly, "I told you I don't own him, and they've been friends since they were small children. He told me that. Besides, you heard him say he doesn't intend to get serious about any girl until he has his medical degree."

"No big deal," she agreed. "He probably has dates lined up for six weeks—all made before he met you. Dennis is a friendly guy."

We talked for a little while longer, then hung up because I heard Mother calling me. Feeling really dismal, I went outdoors to help her bring in the last basket of tomatoes from our garden.

Chapter Nine

Sunday afternoon looked impossibly long and dreary to me. I helped Mother with the tomatoes, did my homework, and practiced my violin, but it seemed as though I'd used practically no time at all. For a few days, life had been so full and so exciting; now it was drab and colorless. Dennis, my mind kept saying, but then it added, Melissa.

I toyed with the idea of straightening up the living room, which was hopelessly messy, but it seemed useless. Justin and his friend Timmy were wrestling on the floor, yelping and squealing and jarring the TV set, which they watched occasionally. In the long front hallway, Michelle and Bonita were racing up and down on their new roller skates. The canner was bubbling away in the kitchen, and there were tomato skins all over the counter. Halfheartedly, I offered to clean them up, but Mother waved me away.

"You've done enough. Go and get some fresh air. Take a walk or visit Amy or something."

"Maybe I'll take a walk," I said listlessly, and she gave me a sympathetic look.

"Do that. It will blow away the cobwebs." She came over and gave me a little kiss on the cheek. "Don't worry, Elizabeth. Things will turn out all right."

I nodded. "Optimist."

I decided I'd rather be alone this afternoon, away from the high-decibel noise in the house, even away from Amy, who would probably feel sorry for me. I went upstairs to comb my hair and put on lip gloss because I don't feel completely dressed without a little makeup. Then I heard the front doorbell ring, heard Bonita's high-pitched little voice and Michelle's cool one talking to our visitor.

"Elizabeth!"

I ran down the stairs, expecting to see Amy or Kim Sutton, but there was a boy standing in our hallway, a boy who was smiling up at me, a boy so tall and lean and lithe that I'd have known him in a crowd.

"Dennis!"

"Hi, Elizabeth. I hope you aren't mad because I came without calling. My car's in the shop, but my father let me take his this afternoon. I've been roaming around, and I thought I'd drop by and see if you're busy."

I'd wanted to see him, dreamed of seeing him,

but now that he was here, I wanted to drop through the floor. The living room, always shabby, was in chaos today, and the two roller skaters were leaning against the wall, obviously ready to skate again as soon as we got out of their way. I introduced them.

"This is Dennis Whitcomb," I said to them, and to him, "My sister Michelle and my sister Bonita." I gestured toward the sea of Sunday papers on the living room rug. "And there is my brother Justin and his friend Timmy." I made a face. "Sorry about the mess. It's the Sunday syndrome at the Ashtons'."

I had to give him credit. He just looked cheerful and interested. "I think it's nice," he said. "When you're an only child, you like to visit people with a big family." He sniffed. "I smell tomatoes. What a great smell!"

"That's chili sauce. Mother's canning again. She's very thrifty. She says we mustn't waste the gifts of nature. Not that the tomatoes are exactly gifts. Mother planted, and we all weeded and watered."

"Am I going to meet the preserver of tomatoes?"

"Sure, if you can stand it. The kitchen looks like a ketchup factory."

He followed me into the kitchen, where my mother sat on a high stool reading a book. Her pretty hair was tied in a bandanna, and there was one thin tomato skin on the end of her nose. She looked up from her book and smiled.

"Mother, this is Dennis Whitcomb."

"Hi, Dennis," she said, and he said hi. They both looked as though they were the people they really wanted to meet that day, if you understand me. That's a quality I admire but don't possess.

"Elizabeth, why don't you get some Cokes and a plate of cookies and take Dennis out on the back porch? The kitchen is stifling, to say nothing of chaotic, but I have to time my canner."

While I got the cookies and drinks, Mother and Dennis started talking like old friends. He asked about her writing, which seemed to fascinate him, and she answered his questions, although usually she doesn't talk about her work. She asked him about basketball and orchestra and about his plans to be a doctor. By the time I had the tray ready and had made Mother a glass of iced tea, they were really chattering away. Mother is a good judge of character, and I knew she liked him.

Dennis and I went out onto the sagging back porch to sit in the sunshine. Immediately we were joined by Figaro and Betsy, who are terrific porch sitters. I liked it because Dennis petted them absently as we talked. I felt as though he liked animals. My mother says people who are good to animals are usually good to children and old people . . . the helpless of this world.

82

After we'd talked for half an hour or so and Dennis had had a ripe tomato from the garden and had admired the pitted, old statue of Pan my mother had bought at a flea market and established in one corner of our small backyard, he asked, "How would you like to go for a ride? My father's car is a lot more dependable than mine, so I like to take advantage of it. Would your mother mind if you deserted her and her tomatoes for a couple of hours?"

"I don't think so. I'll go and ask." Part of me wanted to refuse. Who did he think he was, just dropping in after several days, expecting me to drop everything and go out with him? But another part of me, the romantic part, longed to follow him to the ends of the earth. Call it like, call it love—I was totally attracted to Dennis Whitcomb.

The car was a Lincoln Continental, cream-colored and gorgeous, with every device known to man: air conditioning, automatically controlled windows, plush seats so comfortable you could sleep on them.

"This is beautiful," I said. "I'm surprised your father lets you take it."

"He trusts me." And I could see why. He drove carefully, keeping his eyes on the road. He wasn't a nervous driver, but a really good one. I leaned back and relaxed, wishing only that he would put his arm around me as he'd done in Kevin's car.

When we stopped for a red light, he turned and smiled at me. "I'd like to show you something, a special place. Maybe you won't think it is, but I have a hunch you'll like it. The Ashtons seem to be pretty special people."

I liked that, and it surprised me a bit. I considered the Whitcombs special people but had never stopped to think that to Dennis my family might be extraordinary.

"OK," I said. "Where you lead, I shall follow!"

He liked that. He smiled and pulled away when the light turned green. "It's out in the country a bit . . . about fifteen miles, I guess."

I decided to forget about pride and jealousy and all those ugly emotions and to enjoy the day. I leaned back against the seat and watched the scenery fly by. It was such a golden day, heartbreaking, though, because you knew winter wasn't far off. Already the leaves were beginning to turn, and some were drifting lazily to the ground. We were out in the country now, a different world from Hawkins Street. Here, instead of neat little lawns, there were fields and apple trees laden with fruit. A few horses and cows munched lazily on the abundant grass. A field of corn stalks, a silvery beige color, looked like a setting for Halloween. I loved it, loved the scents of ripening fruit and hay and sunshine coming in the open window.

Finally Dennis turned onto a dirt road, just off the highway. We went up that for perhaps half a mile, and there before us, like the castle in a fairy tale, was a red-brick Victorian house, surrounded by maples and hemlocks, looking still and genteel in the afternoon sunshine.

Dennis looked at me anxiously. "What do you think?"

"Oh, Dennis, I love it! Whose is it?"

He pulled up onto the brick paving stones, just in front of the heavy front door. "It belonged to my grandparents. They're both dead now, but when I was small, I used to spend my summers here, and I loved it. I was always happy here."

He offered me his hand as I got out of the car, and I felt like a girl in a TV commercial: the beautiful car, the fascinating old house and, most of all, the handsome boy.

We went up to the front door, and he pulled a key ring out of his pocket. "Does it still belong to your family?" I asked curiously.

"Actually, they left it to me because they knew how much I loved it. I come out here occasionally and cut the lawn and dust a little, things like that. I have to make it look lived in, to keep the vandals away. Someday, when I'm a doctor and have enough money to restore it and furnish it, I'm going to live here, even if my practice is in the city."

He turned the key, and we went inside. I fell in love with it immediately. The hallway paneling was mellow old wood, and a stained-glass window sent a rainbow of color onto the curving stairway. There was a funny little old-fashioned light on the newel post and a window seat on the landing.

"Come on," Dennis said, catching my hand. "I'm sorry you can't see it with the furniture in it, but we moved that out. Some of it was sold, and some of the antique pieces are at my house. My father said there wouldn't be a stick of furniture left if it remained here. But I'd like to show you the house itself."

He took me into the living room. It had a window seat and a big stone fireplace and more of the walnut paneling that made the hall look so pretty. There were logs in a basket next to the fireplace, and a few had been neatly placed in the fireplace itself. The windows were huge, reaching almost to the floor. Dennis pulled open the shutters on two of the windows, and the late-afternoon sunshine poured in.

"Wait," he said. "I'll light the fire so we can sit in front of it, after the grand tour."

There were three fat cushions in front of the fireplace, and I wondered with a pang if Melissa Cooper had ever sat here with Dennis. But I pushed that out of my mind and watched as he lit the fire, which caught almost immediately. Then, hand in hand, we went through the lovely old house.

The dining room was stately, with old mural-like wallpaper and blue-and-white-painted paneling. The kitchen actually had a butler's pantry with marble counters. The bedrooms were large, with high ceilings, and the bathrooms—two of them—had real tile floors and round marble washbowls.

"There're tea and instant coffee in the kitchen," Dennis said, "and the stove works. I'll put on some water, OK? Can't offer you anything to eat." He grinned. "Good thing your mother fed me so well at your house."

He made us both a cup of tea in blue pottery mugs from the pantry, and we took them into the living room. The fire was blazing by then, and we sat down in front of it and began to talk. In no time at all, I felt as easy with him as I did with Amy or Michelle. I had never found it easy to talk with boys before, but Dennis was so relaxed that I found myself relaxing, too. He was very bright and interested in everything. And he talked about himself, that being an only child had made him happy in some ways and lonely, too, sometimes. That's why he was so fascinated with our family.

"Four seems a lot to me, you know. Of course you could be four nerds, but you're not. You're all good-looking and clever and talented, and that includes your mother."

"My father, too," I said, and realized suddenly how proud it made me to say that. "My father was a professional violinist, but he never became famous. Perhaps if he'd lived longer. . . . Anyway, he made a living by playing second violin in the Civic Orchestra, and sometimes he had to be on the road, and sometimes he had gigs in nightclubs."

"It sounds exciting, not like my family life."

Somehow I didn't mind saying it to him now. "I don't suppose I realized it then, but after my father died, I became aware of just how risky it was. The Civic Orchestra doesn't pay much, and he never wanted to move to a big city, where he might have gotten a seat in a large orchestra. So it was a tight squeeze. Perhaps if my mother had had a job with a salary, it would have been easier, but she's self-employed, too." I was only half-joking when I added, "So you can see why I envy you."

He was giving me a rather strange look. "No, I don't see why. Both my parents are attorneys, and they love it, and I have to admit they make quite a lot of money from it, but that doesn't mean we're any better than your family. We're just different—everybody is different."

I sighed. "I know. But you can see why I've decided not to be a concert violinist or anything like that. I might *teach* music, but even that isn't too likely."

He looked disapproving. "That's a terrible thing to say, Elizabeth. You owe it to yourself to try."

I had to laugh. "I can't believe it—you sound just like my mother!"

He reached over and gave me a mock punch

on the arm. And suddenly, without warning, his arms were around me, and he was kissing me. It was as though someone had opened up a vital vein in my body and released not blood but liquid fire. My whole body seemed to come alive at the touch of his lips.

He was only a year older, but his kisses were much more expert than mine. Even as I clung to him, I was aware of that, aware of his sophistication and of my own inexperience. I could feel my body begin to tremble, feel the warmth from the fireplace like a reflection of the heat within me.

Slowly, reluctantly, he drew his mouth away from mine, and I knew he'd felt the shaking I couldn't control. "The sun's going down," he said in a whisper. Then, in a more matter-of-fact voice, he added, "I promised your mother I'd get you back in time for dinner, and my parents are expecting me by seven. I guess we'd better go."

I couldn't think what to say. I sat up straight, took out my comb and pulled it through my hair, put on lip gloss, tried to smile in Melissa's blasé manner. Then I jumped up. "I'll wash our cups," I said.

We hardly talked as we put out the fire and made sure that every spark was doused with water. Then Dennis locked up, and we got into the car for the short ride back to the city.

On the way back, facing the setting sun, we

talked only a little, and everything we said seemed almost sad. Somehow I knew that we were both retreating from something we couldn't quite handle, and I wondered if today had been the beginning of something, or an ending.

Chapter Ten

The next day I had something more nerve-racking than Dennis Whitcomb to worry about. Even when I thought of our afternoon together, the fire, the old house, and most of all, the kiss, I couldn't quite forget that today was the day of the cheerleader tryouts. Stupid, stupid Elizabeth Ashton, I thought, why did you let yourself in for this? It's much worse than the orchestra audition; at least you can play the violin. You've never shown any aptitude for acrobatics!

"Come with me," I begged Amy at lunchtime. "I can't go through with it without some moral support. I'm so dumb, Amy. I can't do it!"

"Beg off," she said, in her practical way.

"I signed *up*." Then, knowing I could be completely honest with my best friend, I added, "Besides, Melissa Cooper is a cheerleader, and if I don't show up, she'll know I chickened out. I won't give her the satisfaction."

Amy swallowed the last bit of Eskimo Pie. "OK, I'll come with you. But don't say I didn't warn you not to do this, because I did. It's not your thing, Lizbeth."

I said miserably, "I know, but the die is cast, as someone said. I have to go. Three-fifteen, in the gym, OK?"

"OK."

The time went by too fast that day. When you're bored or eager to do something special, the clock hands inch around, but today they flew, and my last class was over. I put my books in my locker and took out my gym suit, wishing we were allowed to wear cute little costumes for the tryouts, so I wouldn't have to wear the shorts and pullover, which were a little large on me and were that ugly shade of green that seems to be used only for gym suits.

Amy was waiting for me at the back of the gym, but she came down front and sat on the bench beside me. About ten girls were trying out, although they only needed three new cheerleaders. I saw Joan Simmons there, sitting with Melissa. I knew Joan was a good friend of Melissa's—and Dennis's, too—and I figured she stood a pretty good chance of making it as cheerleader. She had that casual, smooth air, which is half the battle in life. Surreptitiously I studied her short, black hair, beautiful skin, and small, perfect figure. Completely different from

Melissa, she still had that quality I envied—total self-confidence.

The gym floor squeaked and groaned. And the gym had that barren look and musty smell of gymnasiums in general. Overhead the basketball hoops hung silently, and I thought of Dennis, who was one of the stars of the Parkleigh High basketball team. At any other time it would have thrilled me to think of his running around on this very floor, his tall, lean body poised and ready, his wonderful eyes bright and alert. But today I could think only of the ordeal before me. Last year, at the start of our sophomore year, both Amy and I had been fascinated at the idea of being cheerleaders, although we hadn't been eligible then. But we'd practiced and tried the back flip for weeks in Amy's backyard. We'd glimpsed old Mrs. Bennington watching us from her kitchen window and knew she had had serious doubts about our sanity. But at that time it was only make-believe. Now I was about to put all that self-imposed training to the test—a test I knew I was about to fail.

Mrs. Powers, the gym teacher, said in her chummy way, "Quiet, girls, and let's get going here. I have a meeting at five, and I'm never late, you know." She looks just the way you'd expect a phys. ed. teacher to look: short, sandy hair; a full, oblong face; and a sturdy body kept in beautiful, strong shape by her athletic activities. Her husband is the boys' phys. ed. teacher, and he's not at all what you'd expect: he has a small, thin, wiry body and long curly hair and a sensitive face. He wears frameless glasses and is absentminded, and all the boys say he has no discipline in his classes.

"Joan Simmons," Mrs. Powers called out, and Joan went out into the middle of the gym.

At Mrs. Powers's command, Joan did everything perfectly, as I'd known she would. Her cheers, her back flips, her coordination were as smooth as though she'd been born to be a cheerleader. And probably she had, I thought crossly. Everyone applauded, and it went without saying that she'd made it. I saw Mrs. Powers nod at her approvingly.

Two other girls tried and did fairly well but actually were only mediocre. Then she called, "Elizabeth Ashton."

"Go get 'em!" Amy whispered to me, and I bounced out onto the floor as though I were perfectly sure of myself.

It must have taken all of two minutes to let Mrs. Powers and the rest of the audience know that I wasn't cut out to be a cheerleader. My movements were jerky and self-conscious, and when I tried to do the back flip, I landed on the floor, hurting not only my dignity but also my seat. There was a little flurry of giggles, and when I looked up from my place on the gym floor, I saw Melissa's smile, superior and condescending and sly.

"Want to try again?" Mrs. Powers asked kindly.

I shook my head, afraid to talk because I might cry. My bottom hurt. That floor was awfully hard, and I'd landed hard, too. Even more than that, my pride and my feelings were hurt. It was all so embarrassing. I hated the thought of facing all those girls in classes and in the lunchroom next day. When I do something, I like to do it well, and I'd failed this test abysmally.

On the way home, Amy tried to cheer me up. "You may have made it, Lizbeth. Don't be a defeatist."

I looked her squarely in the eye. "Amy, you're a true friend, but you're a terrible liar. If all the other people were ninety-year-old women, they'd still have done better than I did. And they weren't. Some of them were pretty good. In fact, some of them were great, and that includes Joan Simmons." I added glumly, "And Melissa Cooper would be there to watch. She'll tell Dennis, and he'll think I'm a klutz. Because I am a klutz."

We started to laugh, and finally Amy said, "Why can't you be satisfied being the best violinist at Parkleigh? If I were that good at something, I'd be thrilled."

I sighed. "I guess the truth is, I want to be good at everything, like Melissa and Joan, and like Dennis himself, as far as that goes."

"Well, that's just plain silly. They *can't* be good at everything."

We had come to the corner where we had to branch off toward our own homes. "Go home and practice your violin," she advised. "I'll call you tonight."

When I went into the house, I could smell stew cooking and could hear my mother's typewriter going. I said hello to the cats and to Prentice, got a glass of milk and a handful of chocolate chip cookies, and went up to my room. Looking out my little dormer window, I saw Bonita and Justin and Timmy creating some kind of fort out of a pile of dirt, a couple of kitchen chairs, and two old sheets. I knew they'd be a total mess when they came in, but it looked like so much fun that I couldn't blame them. I remembered the days, not so long ago, when Amy and Michelle and I and some other friends on the block had played just like that. I watched them for a few minutes, listened to their chatter and wished myself a kid again. Had we had troubles then, Amy and I? It seemed to me that our biggest problems had been quarrels between the two of us, a bit of jealousy now and then, when one of us seemed closer to another friend than the other. Or perhaps Amy and I "weren't speaking" for a whole day, and I suffered terribly. By the next day, the quarrel was forgotten.

But this, this longing to be a part of Dennis's group, and worse, the intense embarrassment

96

I'd felt when I'd made a fool of myself at the tryouts, seemed to me like the end of the world.

I sat down on my bed and ate my milk and cookies, realizing that my appetite hadn't been exactly ruined by my misery. I glanced at my homework but decided I deserved a couple hours' respite from school. I took my violin out of its case and glanced through some sheet music. Kreisler, I decided. The things he'd composed had such a lilt. He must have been an optimistic man, or he couldn't have written music like that.

After that, Saint-Saëns, and a little Brahms. No scales today, although Uncle Bob expected me for a lesson tomorrow night. This was a time for self-indulgence, for playing just for the sheer love of the music.

It worked, too. When I put my fiddle away and got ready to go down and help with dinner, I felt somewhat better, although the stinging sense of shame was still there. Suddenly I realized how fortunate I was, to have this gift, this lovely way of transmuting trouble and sorrow—and sometimes fear—into beauty. Did everyone, I wondered, have some way of escaping life's sadness and worries, or was I, as my mother insisted, blessed?

Chapter Eleven

The next morning Mrs. Boland called to say Amy wouldn't be going to school; she'd come down with a cold. That meant going to school without her and, more importantly, eating lunch without her. This was a day when I especially needed her, for I knew the names of the new cheerleaders would be posted outside the gym door, and I knew my name wouldn't be there.

I pushed Justin out the door toward his bus, drank a cup of coffee, mostly to wake me up, and gathered up my books. "Did you eat breakfast, Elizabeth?" Mother called to me.

"Not hungry."

She came to the door. "Elizabeth, how many times have I told you that you can't do a decent day's work without something solid in your stomach?"

"I'm probably getting Amy's cold," I said crossly. I gave her a little peck on the cheek. "See you this afternoon. Hope you get lots of writing done today, Mother."

I was out the door before she could think of any more protests. "Have a glass of orange juice, Elizabeth. Have one slice of toast." She could go on like that for quite a while. Sometimes it was just funny, but today it was irritating, mostly because I was upset about the cheerleading thing. Also, I had hoped Dennis would call me the night before, and he hadn't. I should have been getting used to his sporadic calls, but I kept hoping he might become like other girls' boyfriends—calling every night of the week. Perhaps he'd found me too young and inexperienced and was losing interest.

Glumly I set off on the walk to school. Today it seemed long and boring, although normally I enjoyed it. From kindergarten days, Amy and I had walked to school together. When she'd lived on my block, we'd gone the whole route together, at first accompanied by one mother or the other. Even now I could remember how we'd stopped to gather brown, shiny horse chestnuts on our way home in autumn. Heaven knows what we planned to do with all those chestnuts, but we collected huge bags of them and counted them like misers. Once I made my mother a necklace of horse chestnuts, stringing them together with twine. I found that necklace, dried and dull looking, in her desk only recently, and the sight had brought tears to my eyes because it was a tangible piece of love.

After the Bolands had moved, Amy and I still met every morning at a corner about halfway between our houses and school. Sometimes we walked or rode with friends, but mostly it was the two of us, best friends forever. This morning I especially missed her optimistic way of looking at life. She could always pull me out of the doldrums by pointing out the positive things.

Melissa was only in my French class, for which I was very grateful. She could have been in my history class, as Dennis was, but either she'd taken it the year before or had Mr. Dunwood. If only she hadn't been assigned the early lunch period! Then perhaps Dennis would have sat at our table sometimes. At the very least, I'd have been spared the sight of her perfect face and superior smile. *Why* did she have to look like Brooke Shields? Who wouldn't prefer Brooke Shields to a wholesome, wide-eyed blond like me?

The wind started picking up speed, lifting the leaves on the trees, clanging the sign on Nate's Mobil Station on the corner of Aberdeen and Hillmann streets. I don't like the wind because of its strength, and that day I really feared it because it started to blow me down the street. Waiting for the light to change at Nate's, I hung onto the lamppost for dear life, so the wind wouldn't pick me up and take me down the next block. Just then I heard a horn honking, and someone shouted to me. It was Dennis.

"Get in," he said. "You look as though you're having a war with the wind—and you're losing!"

I got in the car and smiled at him. He really was so *nice*-looking. It wasn't just that he was good-looking; I was brought up not to judge people by their looks and clothes. He really has a niceness about him, and his smile just lights up his face. Any girl would be lucky to have him so much as look at her.

"What are you doing over here at this hour of the morning?" I asked.

"I took my father to the airport. He had to go to Houston on a case, so I took him there and saw him off."

I knew that Dennis's father and mother shared a law office downtown, and I thought that was nice—to be in the same profession, to work together, to have something in common.

"What's new?" he asked.

Suddenly I found myself telling him about the disastrous cheerleading tryouts, and I surprised myself by making it funny! He was a good audience and laughed like crazy at the description of my fall.

"I wish I'd been there," he said.

"Enough people were there to watch me make a fool of myself," I said, remembering the snickers, remembering Melissa's smug look.

"Hey, look," he said, glancing at me sideways,

"anyone who can play the violin the way you do doesn't need to apologize for anything. Being a cheerleader isn't exactly a lifetime career, you know."

"Yeah, but I wanted to make it." I looked at him, half-laughing, half-serious. "Are you sure you don't mind being a friend of a klutz?"

We were pulling into the school parking lot now, and he turned off the motor before he turned to me and said, "Elizabeth, you are not a klutz. And I'd like you if you had two left feet." He took both my hands in his. "How would you like to see me and my two left feet? We're playing West Jonesport Friday night. Would you like to see the game?"

"I'd love to," I said as lightly as though my heart weren't pounding like a jackhammer.

"Great. Look, I'll find out if Kevin and Amy want to go. Then they could take you with them, and we could all go out for hamburgers or something after the game."

We got out of the car then, and I saw a few kids I knew just heading for school. Dennis waved at a couple I knew slightly—Stacey Shaw and her steady Ron Kelly. Even though our meeting had been a chance one, I couldn't help feeling proud because I was with Dennis Whitcomb. It made me feel about ten feet tall, a feeling I really needed today. Despite Dennis's bolstering words, I had a feeling I hadn't heard the last of my dumb performance at the cheerleading tryouts.

I was right. At lunchtime I sat with Kevin, Bob Thrasher, and Jill Warner, but out of the corner of my eye, I saw Dennis and his regulars at their corner table. Melissa was there, of course, and I was amazed at the way she could look so charming and friendly when she was with Dennis and her other friends and so irritating and superior when she was with people she considered beneath her.

They left first, and Dennis said hi to everyone at our table. For the first time, Melissa looked as though she really saw me. She said sweetly; "I'm so sorry you didn't make it as a cheerleader, Elizabeth. Better luck next time."

Dennis sprang to my defense. "I told Elizabeth she should stick to her violin. The orchestra needs her special talents." His tone added that anyone could be a cheerleader. I could have kissed him for that. It gave me the courage to smile back at Melissa just as sweetly—and say nothing. Under normal circumstances, I'd have said something foolish and awkward. Today I realized that silence can be a good weapon.

I had gym fifth period. Until Dennis had encouraged me, I'd been dreading gym, dreading the list on the door, dreading the pitying looks of those who knew I'd tried out for cheerleader. Now, however, I marched boldly up to the door of the gymnasium and read down the list of those who had been chosen. The first name, of course, was Joan Simmons, and by coincidence she was just sauntering down the hall.

"Hey, Joan," I called to her. "Congratulations!"

She turned and smiled at me, almost in surprise, I thought. "Thanks, Elizabeth. Sorry you didn't make it. Better luck next year."

Laughing, I said, "I don't think I'll try again. I don't have your wonderful coordination."

She looked really pleased and thanked me again before she went on down the hallway. I entered the gym, thinking how easy it had been to melt the ice I'd always felt surrounded Joan. Was it really this simple to be friendly with people? I'd always thought of Joan as kind of stuck-up, but she wasn't at all. By complimenting her, I'd broken the ice, and it made me feel good, too.

High on my new-found philosophy—and on Dennis's invitation—I sailed through gym and through my French class. I had something to look forward to now, and that made all the difference.

Chapter Twelve

My family seemed to be showing an unusual amount of interest in my social life, I thought. At dinner Michelle said, "I hear you're going to watch Dennis play basketball."

"How did you hear that?"

"I told her," Justin said, his mouth busy with the chicken casserole.

I scowled at him. "And how did *you* hear it?"

"I heard you telling Mother."

Mother said automatically, "You mustn't eavesdrop, Justin."

"I wasn't. I heard her when I went in to ask if I could go over to Timmy's." He looked hurt because she'd even considered the possibility of his eavesdropping. And of course he hadn't. That's not Justin's style. He's just interested in everything and everyone, in a calm, detached way.

Bonita looked up from her plate. "Do you like Dennis, Elizabeth?"

I could feel my face turning pink. "Sure I like him, Bonita."

She nodded. "I like him. He said he'd like to roller-skate with Michelle and me sometime."

When she said that, I realized that in the short time he'd been in our house on Sunday, he'd made an effort to be friendly to everyone. I realized, too, that he hadn't for one second made me feel uncomfortable about our shabby house. All the discomfort had come from me.

I couldn't wait for Friday and the game, but fortunately I knew I'd see Dennis in history class and at orchestra. Funny how his encouragement had changed my thinking about playing in the school orchestra. That and my successful audition, of course. You win one, you lose one, I thought philosophically, remembering the cheerleading auditions.

The next day at lunch Joan Simmons waved at me across the lunchroom, and I waved back. "Is that you she's waving to like an old friend?" Amy asked in astonishment.

I laughed. "Believe it or not, I congratulated her on being chosen cheerleader, and she really seemed to appreciate it."

Amy sneezed and wiped her nose. "Why not?" she said practically. "Everyone likes to be praised. Why should she be any different?"

I didn't like to tell her that Joan and Melissa and their crowd seemed a world apart from me.

Amy wouldn't understand that at all. I changed the subject. "Kindly get over that cold before Friday, Amy, so we can all go to the game."

"I'll be fine by then," she promised. "But can we go now, Lizbeth? I need to take some aspirin and put on some fresh makeup so I won't look so much like Koko the Clown."

Orchestra rehearsal was fun, but I knew after that first hour that there were only two real musicians there—Jeff Pilato was one, and I was the other. Jeff played the flute and played it like a professional, which I knew he planned to be someday. I played my fiddle like a pro, too. I knew it wasn't my ego speaking; it was my knowledge of music telling me a truth I had never faced before. Jeff and I were professionals playing with amateurs. Mr. Greeley knew it, too. I could tell by the looks he gave me, by the fact that he didn't criticize me, just left me alone to do it right. It gave me a funny feeling. As I've said, I was determined to treat music as a hobby, one that would give me great pleasure, but not my life's work. And here I was, feeling like a pro, not like an amateur at all. It was exciting, and I couldn't help being thrilled, but still I rejected this new feeling.

Dennis and Amy were waiting for me, just standing quietly on the fringe. When I'd finished talking to the others, they came up to me. "See," Dennis said, "I told you you'd be great."

Amy was beaming. "That violin sounded so sweet, Lizbeth. I guess I didn't really know how good you were until now. I wish I'd nagged you into this last year."

Dennis took my arm. "Come on," he said. "Let's you, Amy, and me zip on over to McGillicutty's for a hamburger and shake."

I looked at my watch. "I have to baby-sit for Mrs. Barnes, on my street, starting at six o'clock."

"You can make it," he said. "I'll take you home."

Amy hesitated. "I should go home and nurse my cold." I knew she didn't want to intrude on our date.

Dennis said, "I prescribe a hamburger and a big glass of fruit juice for that cold. Come on, I'll drive you *both* home."

So we went with him and had such a great, relaxing time that I could hardly believe it was Elizabeth the Worrier sitting there in the booth, laughing and joking and, yes, waving to a few kids. I liked the fact that Dennis had urged my friend to go along with us. He kept his arm around my shoulders most of the time, but he made Amy comfortable, too.

Finally we had to go, so that Amy could get home and I could be at the Barneses' house on time. When we pulled up, she was standing on her front porch with little Tommy and Theresa, and I couldn't help being proud because she saw us, saw Dennis reach over and give me a soft kiss on the cheek.

"See you Friday night," he said.

"Friday night."

I thought I'd never live till Friday night, but I did, of course. Amy's cold was better, and she and Kevin picked me up in time to get to Parkleigh to get good seats. West Jonesport High, the visiting team, had a really good standing, and so did Parkleigh, so the gym filled up quickly.

When I saw Dennis lope out in his blue basketball shorts, my pulse leapt. He was tall, although there were some taller players, but to me he looked the most self-assured, the most athletic. It wasn't just my imagination—there was something about Dennis Whitcomb that set him apart from the crowd.

The noise was deafening, and as the game wore on, it got more and more exciting. I'm not exactly the world's greatest sports fan, but I followed every play, cheering for Dennis and the Parkleigh team until I was hoarse. Of course I had to watch Melissa Cooper and the other cheerleaders, but I didn't even care, because I had a date with Dennis after the game. I just yelled and jumped up and down and tried to talk with Amy and Kevin over the din.

At the exciting climax of the game, I was on my feet constantly, and finally I was screaming, "He won! He won!"

Kevin laughed and screamed back, "There were a couple other players in the game, you know!"

"I know, but Dennis was the most important, wasn't he?"

"Sure he was."

After that there was pandemonium, and we couldn't get near Dennis, so we fought our way out of the gym and waited in the hallway for him to change his clothes and meet us. I was so excited that I didn't even get upset when I saw Melissa stop Dennis and say in her high, cool voice, "We're all going over to Peter's house. Come along with us, Dennis, and celebrate your success."

"Sorry, kids, I've got a date. See you soon." And he was on his way to us, leaving Melissa standing there, stunned. If looks could kill . . . but I didn't care tonight. Dennis's date was with me!

It was just about the greatest night of my life. Everything went smoothly. Since Mr. Whitcomb was still out of town, Dennis had his father's car, and, of course, I went with him. We followed Amy and Kevin to Freddy's Place, a big disco.

"I don't see how you can dance after playing basketball for two hours!" I said to him as we danced under the strobe lights at Freddy's Place. I'd never been there before, but I'd heard lots about it, and I found it exciting. The beat of the music, the lights, and the dancers—some of them really terrific—made me feel as though I were whirling through space, whirling like the incredible lights that changed our faces and clothing to unearthly colors.

"I suppose it's because I'm pretty high from the game," he said. "Anyway, this is a different kind of exercise. It's fun, don't you think?"

I think I beamed at him, although I wanted to be cool, as though I came here every week. "I love it. I'm having a great time!"

We went and sat down and had a Coke. Then they began to play a slow piece.

"Want to try it?" Dennis asked. "There's more room for mistakes in this kind of dance. I'll probably step on your feet a few times, but if you're willing to take a chance, so am I."

We instinctively seemed to know how to dance with each other, and he didn't step on my feet once—nor I on his, which was what I'd really been afraid of. I willed my heart not to pound, my body not to tremble, because the feeling of his body so close to mine, his lips on my hair, affected me more than I had ever dreamed possible. Girls dream of this, and they talk about it, but it had never happened to me. When I had turned sixteen in August, I'd still been a child, but now I felt grown up. I wanted that dance to go on and on forever.

111

But of course it didn't. Before I knew what had happened, where I was, the music had stopped, and we were back at the table, sitting with Kevin and Amy, talking. From under my lashes, I looked at Dennis. Had he felt what I'd been feeling, could he possibly be falling in love with me, just a little bit? He was smiling and talking so easily, yet he'd held me very close, and I had felt his kiss on my hair.

"Let's go to the Pizza Palace," Kevin said. "It's a workday tomorrow for us 'menfolk,' and it's getting kind of late."

"Ha," I said. "I'm going to baby-sit all day tomorrow. You think that's not work? The Barnes twins are three years old, and they're holy terrors. What one doesn't think of, the other does. But Mrs. Barnes pays well because hardly anybody will sit for her, except dumb me."

We stayed at the Pizza Palace just long enough to down one large pizza with everything and a soda each; then we decided to go home.

Sitting in Dennis's father's luxurious car, tired but happy, I felt like Figaro when he's had a good meal and he curls up in someone's lap and purrs happily, obviously loving the whole world. It had been such a wonderful evening. After we left the main streets and got onto the quiet side streets where there wasn't much traffic, Dennis put one arm around me in such a casual way that I felt as though I'd known him and loved him forever.

"How about a movie tomorrow night, Elizabeth, just the two of us?" he asked.

"Love to. I only have to baby-sit until dinnertime." Just the two of us. How I loved the sound of that.

"You were great tonight, Dennis, in case I haven't said it before. I don't know how you do so many things so well."

"I don't, really. Jack of all trades, my father calls it."

But he was just being modest. He *was* good at lots of things: sports, schoolwork, social life, dancing. Well, perhaps not quite so good at the clarinet! At that, I had to admit, he was just adequate.

We were on Hawkins Street now, and he said, "Your house is lit up like a Christmas tree. Hasn't your family heard about energy conservation?" Then his voice deepened with concern. "It wasn't like this when we brought you home that other Friday night."

I was ready to jump out of the car. "It never is, unless we have company. I think something must be wrong, Dennis!"

He pulled up to the curb. "Steady. I think I'd better go in with you."

We raced up the front walk, and I pushed open the door. Michelle was sitting on a straight-backed chair in the living room. Her delicate face was chalk white, and when she saw me, she began to cry.

"Michelle! What's wrong?"

Michelle, the cool, the detached one, threw her arms around me. "It's Justin. He was hit by a car, right in front of the house, about eight o'clock tonight. He and Timmy were playing catch, and Justin ran out into the street after the ball. He's in the hospital, and Mother's with him. Someone called an ambulance, and Mother went along in it."

My nails were digging into her arm. "Is he all right? Will he be all right?"

"I don't know. Mother called around ten and said he was in surgery. She told me to stay here with Bonita and wait for you to come home."

I felt so guilty. I'd been out having a good time, while everyone else was miserable. "She should have tracked me down. Did she call Uncle Bob?"

Michelle shook her head. "She said she'd wait until she found out something definite."

Dennis put his arm around Michelle and led her over to the old sofa. "Now you lie down here," he said, putting a cushion behind her. "Elizabeth, get her a blanket. You rest here, Michelle. We'll lock the doors. I'm going to take Elizabeth to the hospital to see your mother and find out what they're doing for Justin. We'll be back in about an hour. Don't let anyone in. Where's Bonita?"

"She's asleep. I put her to bed after Mother called."

Chapter Thirteen

At that hour of the night, the Sterling Memorial Hospital was very quiet. It frightened me to think of my little brother lying somewhere, hurt, perhaps unconscious, and my mother all alone. Dennis went up to the information desk, where a woman was filing visitors' cards and sipping from a green coffee mug.

He talked to her quietly for a minute, then came back to me. "He's in the recovery room. She said we could go in and talk to your mother. We follow the yellow line."

Numb with fear, I walked with Dennis along the hushed corridors, following the endless yellow line that would lead us to the emergency section of the hospital. Occasionally we passed a nurse, and once in a while we heard the muted voice over the loudspeaker, "Paging Dr. Jones. Paging Dr. Wilson."

Finally we pushed open the swinging doors of

the emergency section, and immediately I saw my mother, slumped in a chair, her eyes closed. She sensed our presence, opened her eyes, and her tired face lit up.

"Elizabeth! Dennis!" To my unspoken question she added, "He's all right. A broken ankle; they had to set it, but he's still unconscious from the anesthesia. They told me to go home, but I want to be here when he comes to. It would be just too frightening for him to open his eyes and see hospital walls instead of his own room."

I could easily understand that. When I was five, I'd had my tonsils out, and I remembered opening my eyes in a panic and seeing Mother and Daddy sitting there, smiling at me, reassuring me. "But I could substitute for you, Mother. You look so tired."

She shook her head. "Thanks, dear, but you go home and look after Michelle and Bonita. I know Michelle will be afraid to stay there alone, and it's getting late."

Dennis said gently, "Come on, Mrs. Ashton. We'll all go down to the cafeteria and have a cup of coffee. Then we'll bring you back up here to the waiting room. I'll get you a pillow and blanket so you can lie down on one of the couches. The nurse will call you as soon as Justin is conscious."

Mother acted as though she were glad to have someone thinking for her for a little while. She

117

got to her feet and went down to the elevator with us. We rode to the basement and walked through the silent corridors to the cafeteria, where two or three nurses and a few tired-looking interns sat over their midnight snacks. We seemed to be the only visitors.

"Orders, ladies," Dennis said after he'd seated us.

Mother rallied enough to smile and say, "I've already had one cup of their coffee tonight. I think I'll take a chance on tea."

"A carton of chocolate milk for me, please," I said.

We watched him go over to the counter, take a tray, and begin to pile cups and teapot and milk carton on it. I heard him order cinnamon toast. "You wouldn't believe he played a tough basketball game tonight and went disco dancing after that, would you?" I murmured.

Mother said, "I don't know how he does it, but he looks fresh as a daisy. He's a nice boy, Elizabeth, and a kind one."

He came back, served us efficiently, and when we were finished, guided us back upstairs. It was very quiet now. I felt as though everyone must be asleep, even the suffering ones.

"I want to see Justin," Mother said. "I think they'll let us glance at him, don't you?"

She spoke to the nurse at the desk, and in a few minutes we tiptoed into the recovery room. Under the dimmed lights, Justin lay sleeping, his usually rosy face white and thin, except for the ugly purple bruises on his cheekbones. Even his lips were pale, and he didn't stir. I felt my heart twisting with love for him. In that moment, I knew that what I'd always been told by my mother was right: the only thing that really matters in this world is the happiness and safety of the people you love.

After Mother had leaned over and kissed Justin, Dennis took us to the visitors' waiting room, found a blanket and pillow for Mother, and established her on a leather sofa. At the other end of the room, a man rested on another couch.

"Call me in the morning," I said to my mother, "and tell me how he is. Then I'll come over and sit with him so that you can go home and get some rest."

Dennis and I left the building, his arm around my shoulders in a way I found very comforting. At this moment his touch seemed like that of a big brother, not the thrilling touch of a boy I adored.

When we got home, I said, "Thank you, Dennis. I don't know what I'd have done without you." I tried to smile. "You're a great person."

Without answering, he took me in his arms and kissed me. It was a gentle, reassuring kiss. It was what I needed more than anything at that moment.

"Good night," I whispered.

"I have to work most of the day," he said,

"but I'll be over tomorrow night. If you can't go to a movie, we'll stay here, OK?"

I went on into the house then, tired and ready to cry, but at that moment I loved Dennis Whitcomb even more than I had earlier in the evening.

The next morning everything seemed ordinary and normal again. By the time I'd made breakfast for Bonita, Michelle, and me, Mother had called, telling us that Justin would be all right but would have to stay in the hospital for a few days. When I was ready, without rushing, she said, I could go to the hospital. That would give her a chance to come home, get cleaned up, and rest for a few hours.

"I have to call Mrs. Barnes to cancel my babysitting job. Then I'll call Uncle Bob and Aunt Carolyn," I said. "He was expecting me for a lesson this afternoon."

The day went fast. When I called Aunt Carolyn to tell her about Justin, she started to plan things for us. "If your mother stays at the hospital again tonight, you children must come over here. Uncle Bob will pick you up. You should have called us last night. I don't like the idea of three young girls in a house alone."

I said patiently, "We're all right, Aunt Carolyn. If you want to pick anyone up, bring Mother home tonight after hospital hours. I don't think she'll stay there all night, and I don't like the idea of her coming home by bus after dark."

"You're very thoughtful, dear. We'll take care of it. We want to see Justin, naturally, and take him something to cheer him up."

She would, too. Aunt Carolyn is very generous, in her own way, and I knew she'd take Justin three or four expensive toys and books.

That reminded me. Justin had his book on frogs, a gift from Mother's story sale, but he hadn't picked out one on ancient Rome as yet. I had some baby-sitting money tucked in the black lacquer box on my desk. I'd use that to buy Justin a book. I smiled in anticipation. I knew how to make Justin happy—even with a broken ankle!

I took a bus downtown to buy Justin's book, then I got on another bus, which took me almost to the door of Sterling Hospital. It was lunchtime, and Justin was sitting up in bed, having soup and orange juice.

"Hi, Lizbeth!"

I kissed him and handed him the wrapped package. "Dummy, why did you run out in the street? You're lucky you only have a broken ankle."

He was peeling the bright green wrapper off the book, while Mother and I watched. His face lit up. "Hey, Liz! Thanks a lot! It's just what I wanted."

Mother said goodbye and left, and Justin started looking at the illustrations in his new book. I picked up my paperback and began to read. It was a great mystery, an old Agatha Christie, but I kept losing my place because my mind kept drifting off to Dennis.

When Mother came back about dinner time, all refreshed and bright eyed, I left. "I fed Bonita and Michelle," she said. "I left chicken soup and sloppy joes for you. Be sure to eat. And thanks, Elizabeth."

"Aunt Carolyn said she and Uncle Bob will be here tonight, and they'll take you home, Mother. Wait for them, please."

I wondered if Dennis would come over that evening. I had decided I'd better not go to the movies, even though I knew Michelle could watch Bonita perfectly well. It just seemed a little selfish to go off to a movie when my little brother was in the hospital. And since Dennis had seen the worst of us and still seemed to like me—to like all of us—I thought an evening at our home wouldn't make or break our relationship.

About eight o'clock, he pulled up in front of the house. He was driving his own ancient car this time. I was wearing my best jeans and a white sweater that buttoned up the front to form a turtleneck.

"Hey, you look great!" he said. "Movie or home?"

"Home," I said, "if you don't mind. I'd feel kind of mean leaving Michelle and Bonita here alone under the circumstances."

"Sure. I understand."

It was obvious that Bonita adored him already, and even cool Michelle smiled at him in a much friendlier way than she usually smiles at me.

"Do you want to roller-skate, Dennis?" Bonita asked.

Dennis hesitated, and Michelle said firmly, "He isn't here to entertain you, Bonita, he's here to visit Lizbeth. Go watch TV or read a book or something."

Bonita looked downcast, as only Bonita can, and Dennis said quickly, "Find something to do for a while, Bonita. Then before your bedtime, we'll all go out and have a great big ice cream cone. How does that grab you?"

Her whole tragic face came to sudden life. "It grabs me great!" Without another word, she whirled off into the living room and turned on the TV.

"I'll watch with her," Michelle said graciously and followed Bonita.

Dennis and I looked at each other. "You're going to make a great doctor," I said. "Why not be a psychiatrist? You know how to handle people."

He shook his head. "Pediatrician. So I'll need to know how to handle children."

"Want to sit on the back porch?" I asked. "It's not too cold outside, and it's still sort of pretty."

We went outside and sat and watched the moon come up over the trees on the next street.

We held hands, and we sat very close together, and I was happy. I decided not to think about anything except this moment. Dennis might never become my steady boyfriend, but he was here now, and he seemed to like my companionship.

We talked about everything. Until now I'd never been able to think of things to say to boys. My tongue could run with the speed of sound when I was talking about something to one of my girlfriends—particularly Amy—but I'd always been a little tongue-tied with boys. Dennis and I were compatible. That's a word my mother often uses, and that's what Dennis and I were. We understood each other. On many subjects we had the same opinions, and even when we disagreed, it was fun just sharpening our wits, pretending to argue, pretending to be angry.

And all the time we sat there, side by side, close together, my body was saying things it had never said before. These feelings were new and a little frightening. Mother's little talks, even those sex education classes in school, hadn't really prepared me for this all-consuming feeling of desire. Did Dennis feel it, too? I couldn't tell, for his kisses were casual, not demanding. I thought this might be because he knew I wasn't nearly as experienced as he was.

Pretty soon he looked at his watch in the faint light of the moon and said, "It's nine o'clock. We'd better take Bonita out for that ice cream before she falls asleep, don't you think?"

The four of us got into Dennis's car and went to Spanky's, way across town, for the best frozen custard in the area. Bonita kept beaming at us as she licked the huge ice cream cone. "I wish we had a car," she said. "This is the best food I've had for a whole week or more!"

We were sitting in Spanky's parking lot, eating the ice cream, and Dennis bowed to her over the backseat. "Madame," he said, "I am your willing slave. Just call on me when you get the hungries for custard, and I shall whisk you away in my chariot and buy you ice cream."

Bonita giggled, and Michelle said dryly, "Be careful. She'll take you up on that. She never forgets a promise."

"I mean it," Dennis said. To me he added, "I expect you to let me know when your little sister needs a custard fix."

"Sure," I said happily. That sounded like the offer of someone who intended to stick around.

After the trip for ice cream, we went back home. Mother had just been dropped off by Aunt Carolyn, and she looked relaxed and cheerful.

"Justin will have to be in the hospital for a few more days," she said, "but at least there are no internal injuries. He's young, and the doctor says his ankle will heal fairly quickly, even though it was a bad break."

"I'll take Elizabeth to the hospital from school on Monday," Dennis said, "and bring you home, if that's all right with both of you." He grinned at my mother. "Tell Justin I'm coming in to check him over, to get some practical experience before I ever get to medical school."

Mother put her hand on his arm in a gentle, confiding way. "Dennis, you're a very kind boy, and you're going to be a wonderful physician. You have all the right qualities."

He blushed a little, the first time I had seen that in confident Dennis, but I could tell he was pleased. To me he said, "Do you want to make the late show, or are you tired out by now?"

I hesitated. "Let's play some backgammon and have some of the famous Ashton hot chocolate and save the movie for some other time."

"Sure," he said, and I got out the backgammon board.

I could hardly believe that I was talking to him as casually as Amy did to Kevin. It just felt right, somehow, and once again I hoped that eventually Dennis might consider me his special girl. College and medical school were so far off. . . . Surely he wouldn't mind committing himself to someone, just for his high-school days?

Chapter Fourteen

Dennis said he would have relatives visiting on Sunday and that he had to be home all day, so I knew I wouldn't see him. But I lived on the memories of Friday and Saturday nights. It was enough to sustain me. And I knew I'd see him on Monday after school.

I rushed around the house making meat loaf and soup and things so that there wouldn't be so much to do during the week. I was emulating Mother, I realized. I hadn't known that I was watching her so closely over the years, but somehow things seemed to fall into place in her absence. Michelle and I cleaned the house, without a word of argument from either of us. I suppose we were just so glad to have Justin safe and alive that it didn't seem worthwhile to fight. Besides, I kept thinking of Dennis, and that kept me happy.

Uncle Bob called. "Since you missed your lesson yesterday, Elizabeth, how about my stopping there and giving you one? I can take your mother to the hospital afterward, if she hasn't left already."

So that afternoon I set up my music stand in the dining room and closed the door on Bonita and her friend Tracy, and Uncle Bob and I got to work. He knows the violin, knows exactly how things should be, and knows when I make the tiniest of errors. When he tucks that fiddle under his chin, to show me how a passage should go or where my fingering is wrong, I know that I'm watching an expert.

"Uncle Bob, don't you ever wish you'd tried to be a professional violinist?" I asked now.

He laid my violin down carefully. "Sometimes," he admitted. "No guts, I guess, Elizabeth. Your Aunt Carolyn and I have a good life. I'm content. I suppose if I'd really wanted to make it in music, I'd have tried, as your father did."

He didn't have to say it. Aunt Carolyn would never have put up with an uncertain life-style like ours. She had had several secretarial jobs when she was younger, and now she was secretary to the president of a big company. She liked a well-ordered life. Everything in her kitchen, for example, matched, and her life was like that.

"You're right, of course," I said. "It's just that you're so talented, I wondered why you never tried."

"Well," he said cheerfully, "I did what you're doing—played in school orchestras, played with a chamber quartet when I was in college. Let's call music my hobby, not my life's work."

I didn't press the issue. I had a feeling it made him a little uncomfortable to be asked about his musical ability.

I fixed lunch for Uncle Bob and the others, then he and Mother went off to the hospital. I washed my hair, did my homework, practiced my violin, took Bonita to the park for a while, and still had time left over. I had resigned myself to not hearing from Dennis. After all, family came first. Besides, today's guests, he had told me, were his mother's parents and his aunt and uncle, and he was close to all of them. But about nine o'clock the phone rang.

"Hi, Elizabeth. How's our wounded hero today?"

"He's coming along fine, thanks. How was your day?"

"Great. I love to see my grandparents. They're super. They live about three hours away, so I don't see them too often. My dad's parents are dead—they're the ones who had the brick house. So I figure I'd better hang on to the ones I have left."

"I know. Until my father died, I thought people close to you lived forever." I gave a nervous little laugh. "But it ain't true."

We talked for quite a while, at first seriously

about losing people you love, then about a book we both happened to be reading, then just silly stuff. Dennis, I'd found out, was really good at off-the-wall, zany humor. He'd just go into it sometimes, so that at first you thought he was saying something serious—but then you'd realize he was being a complete and utter nut.

Finally he said, "I guess I'd better go finish my homework. I didn't get any of it done today. See you tomorrow afternoon, out in the parking lot, OK? I'll take you to the hospital, then take your mother home. And I want to take a present to that little turkey!"

I hung up and sat hugging my knees, reliving every moment of our talk. I knew I wasn't wrong about one thing: Dennis was a really nice person. Trouble was, practically every girl at Parkleigh thought so, too.

The house was quiet. Michelle was doing her homework in her room. I'd helped Bonita get ready for bed just before Dennis called. It seemed strange not to hear Mother's typewriter going— strange and lonely. I knew she'd be home soon, but I missed her. I was used to her reassuring presence, used to her absentminded but somehow efficient way of running things at home. She might forget to turn off the gas under the soup kettle sometimes, but she never forgot a hurt or bump, never neglected us or the animals. For the first time, I realized my mother might be right: it was good that she could work

130

at home, especially now. She'd be right here when Justin came home, and she didn't have to ask for time off in order to visit him at the hospital. When Amy had had pneumonia last year, Mrs. Boland had been frantically worried about Amy and had taken her personal days to be with Amy when she was her sickest. I could see how hard these things could be on a mother.

The next morning, flying around the kitchen, trying to get breakfast for everyone so Mother could have an extra hour's sleep, cleaning up the table and counter, finding Bonita's sweater and making her lunch—no cafeteria in the elementary school—I thought how hard it must be to be a full-time mother. Filling in for just a few days had made me aware of the fact that it was a hard job. By the time everyone was out the door and I'd awakened Mother, I was ready to leave the house, too, but I also felt frantic and irritable.

I rushed off to meet Amy, who took one look at me and said, "What tornado hit you? You forgot to comb the back of your hair, and you don't have any eye makeup on, and you look right off the wall."

I gave her a filthy look. "Can't you think of anything else that's wrong with me? There's nothing like a little support."

Amy laughed good-naturedly. "Sorry, I didn't mean to hit you while you're down. What's up?"

"Just feeling sorry for myself, I guess. I tried

to get Bonita and Michelle off to school and get things in order for dinner tonight because there won't be much time to do it after school." Then, remembering, I smiled. "Dennis is going to pick me up after our last class and take me to the hospital and give Mother a ride home."

Amy looked at me. "I should think you'd be as happy as anything. What more could you want?"

I was tucking in my blouse and running a comb through my hair as we walked along, scuffing our feet through the early leaves. The air was wonderful this morning, so crisp and clear. It was impossible not to feel good on a morning like this, and my mood changed.

"I get mean when I have to hurry around. I always figure I won't be ready on time."

"But you always are," she pointed out. "If anything, you're usually a little ahead of time."

"I know." I smiled at her. "I guess I'm just compulsive, whatever I'm doing. Amy, isn't Dennis nice? Isn't he sweet?"

Despite the hurrying, the worry over Justin, and the fact that it was costing money we didn't have, the next couple weeks went by like a dream. Justin came home within a few days and was propped up on the couch in the living room. In no time he was swinging along on his crutches as though he'd had them for years.

"Look, Ma, no hands!" he would shout to Mother as he swung along, hands outstretched, the crutches somehow tucked under his arm-pits. Every time he did it, Mother would cringe, but he never fell, despite the heavy, hip-high cast.

I loved the fact that Dennis stopped in so often, sometimes after school, sometimes after basketball practice. Often he stayed only ten or fifteen minutes, but he usually brought some little thing for Justin: a magazine, a tiny collec-tion of gemstones from the museum shop, a chinese checkers game he'd found at a flea market, a terrarium, and one day a big box of Fanny Farmer chocolates, which made Justin's eyes huge.

The only trouble was that Dennis began to seem like a member of the family, and not like my boyfriend. Was this how he resolved his conflict about girlfriends and staying unin-volved—by just being friendly? When he came to the house, he would sometimes give me a little kiss, but it was a kiss he could just as easily have given Bonita or Michelle. It was noth-ing like the kisses we'd exchanged that day at the old brick house. Then I'd thought he might be falling in love with me, but with each pass-ing day, I began to think that less and less. Perhaps because I'd pulled back from his kisses that bright Sunday, he thought of me as a kid. Would Melissa pull back, or Joan, or any one of those other pretty, sophisticated girls? Not in a million years.

On the first Saturday night after Justin came home from the hospital, Dennis dropped in, without having asked me for a date. After he'd talked to the younger children and my mother for a while, he asked, "Want to see a movie, Elizabeth? We never did get to the one the night after Justin was hurt."

I felt a little cool, but I said, "Sure. Wait till I change."

He looked me over. "You're OK. Why change? That outfit looks great on you."

"That outfit" was a jump suit I'd bought when they first came out. It was pretty old, and I'd never really liked its shade of green, but I'd worn it a lot because I couldn't afford to throw away money. Under it I wore a white blouse of Aunt Carolyn's, which had happened to fit me instead of Michelle. I looked, I thought, like your average chimney sweep. If Dennis wanted to take me out looking like this, then he didn't really see me, and I found that very depressing.

I went into the bathroom and combed my hair and put on fresh makeup. You're an idiot, Elizabeth Ashton, I thought. You wanted to be on easy, friendly terms with Dennis. Now you don't want to be. But the truth was, I thought Dennis was coming to our house to see the whole Ashton family, whom he obviously adored, instead of just me. And I was jealous, plain old jealous.

Chapter Fifteen

Things went on in pretty much the same way for a while. The days went by quickly, like the leaves that floated to the ground each day now, faster and faster, pretty but fleeting. Dennis came to our house a lot, usually with some little offering for Bonita and Justin. Often he took us out for what he always called "a custard fix," and this was a real treat for everyone. I knew my mother adored him, and that meant a lot, since I adored him, too. I didn't think he was dating his other girlfriends very often; he didn't have time. But we did a lot of double-dating with Amy and Kevin, and I had the feeling he wasn't mad about being alone with me. He had his eye on the future, and he was strong enough to remember his goals. He didn't have to tell me that again. It showed.

One thing that bothered me: Dennis never changed his lunchroom habits. He still ate lunch with Melissa and Brad and Joan and Dusty, all members of his own crowd. Sometimes he'd stop and chat with Amy and Kevin and me, and anyone else who sat at our table, but it was always casual. Certainly it never made me feel as though I were special, particularly when Melissa stood there, her nose in the air, as though she couldn't wait for Dennis to stop talking to the peasants.

If we ran into kids we knew when we were out, I did feel special, though. Some of them, I thought, were seeing me for the first time. They noticed me now and looked at me with respect. Those who were in the school orchestra treated me as someone special, too, and I knew Mother would say this was more important, for it was something I'd achieved on my own. I knew she'd frown at the idea of my being accepted because of Dennis's popularity, so I didn't mention it to her.

One night about two weeks before Halloween, Dennis and I were playing backgammon in my living room, and he said, "I'm thinking of giving a Halloween party at my grandparents' house on Hilton Road—the house I showed you. What do you think? It seems like a good, spooky setting for Halloween, doesn't it? We could all go in costume."

"Sounds neat. And the house will be perfect. I think it's beautiful, Dennis, and mysterious." In my uncertain moments, I would take out the memory of our afternoon at that house and linger over it. The mellow red brick, the dormer windows of the exterior, and the beautiful paneling and floors inside made it seem like a fairy-tale house to me. And the thought of those hours in front of the fireplace were half-wonderful, half-painful. I wondered if he thought about that day, but his eyes met mine very openly, no different, as I saw it, from the way they met Michelle's.

"I'll have to get busy," he said, "cleaning up and planning the food and stuff. I think I'll make it an old-fashioned Halloween, the kind my grandparents have told me about—ducking for apples, maybe, square dancing, cornstalks around the room. If it's too corny for anybody, that's their tough luck." I could see he was getting more and more enthusiastic as he talked.

"If you need help, just call on me," I said, and marveled that I was able to say that. A month ago, I wouldn't have had the nerve.

"Thanks, I may do that."

As it turned out, I had to baby-sit for Mrs. Barnes the following Saturday when Dennis started to get things ready for his party. "I'm sorry you can't come along, Elizabeth," he said. "A bunch of us are going out to get things ready."

I tried to be light about it. "Can't be helped," I

said. "Duty and money call. Mr. and Mrs. Barnes are going out of town for the weekend. Think of me with those twins and pity me!"

"I'll think of you every minute and wish you were there." How I ached to have him mean it. I would have given my right arm to be there with the rest of "the bunch," but Fate had stepped in, I guess, and I was trapped with the Barnes twins.

I didn't see much of Dennis that week, except for a minute at lunchtime and at orchestra practice. We talked for a little while after that, and he told me things were going well for the party, moving along.

"Have you decided what you're going to wear?"

"Nothing very clever, I'm afraid. I'm not too good at sewing. But since it's an old-fashioned party, I thought I'd wear a long dress and sunbonnet—Mother's making me one out of the same material as the dress. And if you don't mind, I thought I'd take my violin. If you need some old-time square dance tunes, I think I could play a few."

He grabbed my face in both of his hands and kissed me squarely on the nose. "That would be super, Lizzie Ashton! Practice up your hillbilly tunes, and I'll make a poster: Entertainment by Lizzie Ashton, the Famous Fiddler."

"Not the *only* entertainment!" I protested.

He said easily, "One of my mother's friends plays the piano pretty well. She's Alicia Fortunata. She'll be there."

I gasped. Alicia Fortunata is a famous musician. She lives in our city part of the time—when she's not off on a concert tour.

"Got any more of those unknowns to play for your party?"

He laughed. "I've got Elizabeth Ashton, who *will* be a famous musician. And my dad says he remembers *his* father used to call for barn dances in the old days, so Dad might try those."

"I don't think I dare play in the same room with Alicia Fortunata," I said. "I'd be petrified."

"You can do it. Remember what I said about having faith in yourself."

I tried to remember it all weekend, while I sat with the Barnes twins and tried to keep them from killing each other. After they were in bed on Saturday night, I moped around thinking of all the fun Dennis and his friends must be having at the red brick house, getting it ready for the party. I would have given a lot to be there.

Amy called me. Kevin was at her house, watching TV with her. Dennis obviously hadn't invited them to help out, although he'd invited them to the party.

"I suppose Melissa is there, running the show," I said to Amy.

"Boy, you really sound down," she said. "I thought things were going pretty well between you and Dennis."

"I suppose so. But at a time like this, I wish I were there, covering my territory." I added gloomily, "If it *is* my territory."

Amy said impatiently, "Lizbeth, you never used to be so unsure of yourself—not until you fell in love! You used to take things as they came."

"I know, but there was never anything I wanted so badly before this. Amy, how does any girl ever take a boy for granted, a boy she really likes?"

There was a second's hesitation. "Well, I can hardly express myself freely right now!"

I'd forgotten Kevin must be there somewhere in the background. I could hear the TV. "Sorry, I forgot. But you can answer yes or no. Do you feel sure of Kevin? You certainly act as though you do."

"Pretty sure, I guess, but then it works both ways, doesn't it?"

"You mean you think boys aren't always sure of their girlfriends?"

"Well, of course not. They're human, too, Lizbeth!"

That gave me something to think about, so I switched off the TV, which was boring, and got to work on my costume for the party. The Barneses' sofa was more comfortable than ours, so I curled up there and did the tiny hem-stitching that would make this piece of cotton

140

look like something my great-grandmother had worn, many years ago. The material was a soft cotton with a white background and tiny, tiny blue nosegays. Mother and I had made the dress together on the old pedal sewing machine, which had belonged to Grandma Ashton. I would have hated to have Aunt Carolyn look at the seams, but for a costume, I thought it would be fine. When I'd finished hemming, I went into the bedroom, which had a full-length mirror on the back of the door, and tried on the dress.

My hair is pretty long; it's straight and blond, about the color of corn silk. I didnt' want to braid it, so I swept it up on the top of my head and fastened it with Michelle's silver barrette. I looked at the figure in the mirror for a long time. The girl in the mirror was a romantic, dreamy figure; someone, I thought, who looked sure of herself at last, sure that a boy like Dennis could really like her. I went back to the living room, where I had stashed my violin case out of the reach of the terrible twins. Then I went back to the long mirror.

When I lifted the violin and drew the bow across the strings, I looked like the youngest violinist in a symphony orchestra. A musician, pure and simple. It shook me a little, but I said to myself, "Just because you look like a professional violinist doesn't mean you're fit to be

141

one. Stop thinking about it, Elizabeth. You've made up your mind to be a practical person. Stick to your ideas."

But when I practiced the violin softly, as the twins slept, I couldn't help picturing myself on a stage, somewhere, sometime.

Chapter Sixteen

Dennis called me at the Barneses' Sunday afternoon. "Everything's just about ready," he said, "except the food. We decorated with cornstalks and pumpkins and Indian corn, and it looks nice and old-fashioned, I think."

I couldn't quite make myself ask him who "we" were, but I could guess. It hurt to think that he just naturally turned to his old friends to help him get ready for the party, but it was understandable. I simply couldn't be reasonable about Dennis. I guess I wanted him all to myself.

"I'll be out there with my parents Saturday night," he said, "getting everything under way. My mother's making tons of food, of course, enough for a small army, but we have to carry it out along with some folding chairs and cushions and stuff. Is it OK with you if Kevin and Amy pick you up and take you out?" He put on a pompous tone. "As host of this old-time barn dance, I must be there early to greet my distinguished guests."

"Sure," I said. I'd have felt much happier if he'd asked me to go with him and help out, but I couldn't very well say that. I felt vaguely unhappy and unwanted, although I knew that was silly. He had asked me to his party, he'd asked me to play with Alicia Fortunata. What more could I want?

When we drove up to it, the house looked like a Gothic mansion. Grinning jack-o'-lanterns were in the windows, and they gave an eerie light. Amy and I giggled a little nervously. It was spooky.

"This is fabulous!" Amy said to me. "No wonder you flipped over it. Imagine owning this!"

Dennis came to the door to greet us. He was dressed like Daniel Boone, and he really looked smashing. He greeted Kevin and Amy, and to me he whispered, "You look beautiful!"

He took us into the big living room to meet his parents, who were standing with a small group of grown-ups. Mrs. Whitcomb was dressed in a blue satin outfit, with many layers of material over real hoops, and Mr. Whitcomb looked distinguished in a dark velvet suit and a powdered wig, which made him look like Alexander Hamilton.

"So this is Elizabeth!" Mrs. Whitcomb said. "I've heard a lot about you, and I must say, you

144

live up to your description. I hear you're going to play the violin for us later."

"Well, I thought just some square dance tunes," I said, my voice barely audible. I wished I had never agreed. Hadn't I promised myself to play only for my own pleasure and that of my family? Even the school orchestra was a big concession, but this was worse. These were adults who would be judging me. Including Alicia Fortunata.

"Come over to the fire and have some hot cider," Mrs. Whitcomb said, putting her hand on my arm. She was very pretty, her blond hair in an elaborate hairdo.

Mr. Whitcomb seemed just the right husband for her. He had strong, handsome features, very like Dennis's, and he was tall and impressive. For a minute, right there among all those laughing people, I wanted to burst into tears. The Whitcombs looked so relaxed, so attractive, so much at ease, and I knew their air of careless well-being was due, at least in part, to their comfortable circumstances. Somewhere inside me I felt a terrible pain. I wanted my mother to be able to live like this. She was pretty and funny and talented, and she would shine in this kind of gathering. Instead, she was at home, worrying about Justin, worrying about money, worrying about college for four kids.

I pushed the thought to the back of my mind, however, and took my cup of hot mulled cider and wandered around with Amy and Kevin, talking to the kids we knew. Melissa, I noted with a thrill of relief, wasn't there, or at least not yet.

The apple-log fire blazed in the huge stone fireplace, and the wood smoke mingled with the smell of apples—bushels of them—which sat on old, wooden benches in the corners of the living room. There was a faint aroma of cinnamon, too, from the cinnamon sticks in the mugs of cider. The sound of voices grew into a small roar.

Pretty soon Dennis stood in the center of the room and said, "Let's duck for apples—a prize for anyone who manages to snare one with his teeth!"

Everyone watched as the apples were dropped in tubs of water; then we took turns bobbing for them. I hadn't done that since our third-grade Halloween party at school, and I was surprised at how difficult it was to capture one.

Dennis was beside me now. "This is fun!" I said, gasping, my face wet from the apple tub.

He was puffing like a porpoise. "Challenging, too, isn't it?"

I nodded, plunged in again, and speared one with my front teeth. As I came up for air, triumphant, I saw Melissa come in with a dark, good-looking boy who looked old enough to be a college freshman. Well, at least she was with a date, I thought thankfully.

"Oh, there's Melissa with Dave Barry," Dennis said and went loping off to greet them. He didn't look in the least upset, but I wasn't sure how to take that. Either he was very sure of her, or she really was just his longtime friend, as he'd said.

The Whitcombs were sitting with a half-dozen other adults on folding chairs before the fire. Now Mrs. Whitcomb got up and brought over a small, graceful woman with dark hair parted in the middle and a great deal of eye makeup. "This is Dennis's talented friend, Elizabeth Ashton," she said. "And this is Alicia Fortunata."

"How do you do," I said, my voice fading to a whisper.

Miss Fortunata laughed. "Don't be shy, dear. I'm anxious to hear you play."

Trapped, I looked at Mrs. Whitcomb. "I thought—just for the square dancing?"

"Well, I promised to do that, too," Miss Fortunata said, "but first, shall we try—what?—something simple but lovely. Brahms's 'Lullaby.' Do you know that from memory? It may not be appropriate so early in the evening, but who cares?"

Mrs. Whitcomb said something to her husband, and he held up a hand for silence. Then he said, "Before we start the dancing, we have a real treat in store for us. Miss Alicia Fortunata, the famous pianist, and a talented young violinist, Elizabeth Ashton, will play Brahms's 'Lullaby' for us."

I was shaking like a leaf. The room was full of faces, all of them watching me. I felt the kids might be bored, even by a great artist like Miss Fortunata, let alone Elizabeth Ashton, who was just your ordinary, average high-school girl. The members of the school orchestra had applauded me, but after all, they liked music; that's why they were in the orchestra. But many of Dennis's friends, I felt sure, would despise classical music.

I looked over at the far end of the room, and there, seated on a big floor cushion, was Melissa Cooper, surrounded by boys, of course, and looking at me with the faintest of sneers. She was hoping I'd mess this up. That did it. I followed Miss Fortunata to the piano, a spinet that had been moved from Dennis's house just for the evening, and picked up my violin. When I heard her opening notes, I knew I could play. She was so skilled, her piano playing so beautiful, that I forgot myself and followed along.

When we finished, there was real applause. I ducked away, so Miss Fortunata could take a bow, but she caught my hand and drew me beside her. "Dennis was telling the complete truth, my dear. You really can play. Who is teaching you?"

"My uncle."

She raised her eyebrows but said, "He must

148

know the violin very well. I shall speak to Mr. Greeley at your school. He's a friend of mine. I think he could arrange something for you."

I didn't know exactly what that meant, but I thanked her and backed away from the adults and went looking for Kevin and Amy.

Dennis found me first. "You were great, Elizabeth. I feel really pleased with myself for pushing you along!"

"You probably pushed me into a slight nervous breakdown, Dennis Whitcomb!"

He caught my hand and pulled me toward the piano. "The corny entertainment is about to begin. So pick up that fiddle again."

In a few minutes the square dancing began, and Miss Fortunata played songs like "Turkey in the Straw" with lots of verve, bouncing on the piano stool like a teenager. Dennis's friend, Joe Haggerty, had brought his guitar, and I sawed away at the fiddle, like a real country-and-western performer. Mr. Whitcomb was the caller, and a pretty good one, too. He had a nice, clear, mellow voice and seemed to know all the calls. It was fun, and the music was lively, and everyone was swinging around the room like crazy. I loved it all but began to wish I could try the dances, too. I felt like a paid performer, someone being tolerated because she could entertain.

About then, as though reading my mind, Dennis came over to me and said, "Joe can fill in for a while. Come and dance. You'll love it."

I did enjoy it, but it was nothing like that night at the Cowpoke, when he had held me in his arms to the slow dance, and I had felt his tender kiss on my hair. This was all noise and "allemande left" and dozens of feet thumping over the polished wooden floor. It was spirited and really exciting, but I longed desperately to have Dennis at my side for the evening. I wanted to feel special again, to be his girl, at least for the course of this important evening.

As soon as the set was over, however, he said, "See ya," and went off to help his mother and a couple of her friends set up the refreshments in the dining room. Desperately I looked around for Kevin and Amy, who were my only real friends there, other than Dennis himself. I wanted to dash around and talk to everyone, even acquaintances, but I couldn't do it without the bolstering of someone like Amy or Dennis.

"Hey, Lizbeth!" It was Amy calling from across the room. She and Kevin came toward me.

"Food!" Kevin said. "Let's go get it."

The dining room was set with folding tables, which were decorated with bright paper tablecloths and napkins and bunches of gourds and Indian corn. It all looked so festive. If I hadn't had this miserable, sinking feeling in the pit of my stomach, I'd have admired all the clever little touches. They were probably Melissa's touches, anyway, I thought morosely. I'd heard she was a good artist.

The refreshments were great: hamburgers and pizza and more cider and apple pie and doughnuts. Kevin piled his plate high and beamed at Mrs. Whitcomb. "Good stuff!" he said. "All my favorites."

Mrs. Whitcomb said, "I suppose pizza isn't really suitable for a country party, but it seemed necessary for teenagers." She smiled at Kevin. "I'm so glad you like my choices."

Melissa had just come up to the table. "It's perfect, Mrs. Whitcomb. Everything is perfect." She smiled prettily at Dennis's mother. I noticed she didn't tell me I was perfect, nor my music! In fact, she acted as though I weren't even there.

I edged away. Mrs. Whitcomb was being nice to me because I was Dennis's friend, but Melissa, I knew, was like a daughter to her. Dennis had told me that the Coopers and Whitcombs were lifelong friends, and it was obvious that Melissa was very comfortable with the Whitcombs. I was an imposter, a fiddle player in this world that was not for me. This was Melissa's world—and Dennis's—not mine. Mine was the world of Hawkins Street, where the kitchen linoleum was wearing thin, and the living room sofa was sagging.

Pretty soon Amy came up to me and said, "Kevin is about ready to go home, Elizabeth. Are you coming with us or waiting for Dennis?"

"I'll come with you," I said quickly. "Just wait till I say goodbye to the Whitcombs and to Dennis."

I said good night to Mr. and Mrs. Whitcomb and to Miss Fortunata, then found Dennis talking to some of the other kids from Parkleigh. "Amy and Kevin have to go, Dennis. They'll give me a ride home."

He smiled at me. "I'm sorry you have to leave. But thanks for the beautiful music, Elizabeth. You were great, and you look wonderful. I'll call you, OK?"

"OK." I went to get my violin. I couldn't have said one more word without crying. I knew he couldn't leave now, just to drive me home, but I longed for him to ask me to wait till the party was over, so he could take me home, so we could have one sweet good-night kiss, one little sign that I was his girl. But I wasn't.

As we left I turned around for one backward glance at the candle-lit room, and there, before the fireplace, her skirts spread gracefully about her, was Melissa, smiling at her date, Dave Barry, then turning to smile much more brilliantly at Dennis Whitcomb.

Chapter Seventeen

The next day was a lost day. My brief romance with Dennis Whitcomb was over, I knew that. A girl just knows these things. All along, he had been so friendly and warm and comfortable with my family and my friends Amy and Kevin, but on his home ground, he had been so different. To the Whitcombs I was Dennis's little friend Elizabeth—no more than that, his friend. And obviously that was the way he felt about me, too. I knew, honestly, that he wasn't madly in love with Melissa or anyone, but I also knew that someday, when he allowed himself to get serious about a girl, it would be about someone like Melissa—if it wasn't Melissa herself. She had belonged with his parents and friends, and with Dennis himself, and she'd made that very clear to me.

Mother fussed over us, as she always does on

Sundays. She made french toast with maple syrup especially for Justin.

"That's all you're getting until dinner tonight," she said cheerfully, as we were sitting around the table. "Unless you want to fix yourselves sandwiches. I'm going to put a small turkey in the oven for tonight." She looked at me sharply. "Why aren't you eating, Elizabeth? You love french toast."

"I'm not hungry."

Michelle groaned and clutched her forehead. "Oh, oh, when Lizbeth isn't hungry, it means she's having a problem. What's your problem, Liz?"

"Shut up," I said.

"Girls." Mother looked at me again. "Is something wrong, Elizabeth? You do look a little pale. Didn't you have a good time last night?"

"It was OK. We had square dancing."

"Well, that sounds like fun. Did you play the violin? Did everyone like your costume?"

"Sure." I wasn't going to say anything when Michelle was watching like a vulture, ready to snap me up.

Mother didn't say anymore until Michelle went off to the movies with her friend Sharon. Then she called to me from the kitchen. "Elizabeth, come and help me get this turkey into the oven, will you?"

It wasn't a very big turkey, and I knew she could have lifted it herself easily, but I also

154

knew she was trying to get me away from Justin and Bonita, who were playing a game in the living room, so she could talk privately.

"Make us a cup of tea," she said, "while I peel the potatoes. I like to have everything ready, so I can just pop them on the stove at the right time."

Silently I made the tea, in a pot today, not just with tea bags, because I knew she would take time to sit down and have two or three cups. I put out the cups, sliced a lemon, and put out the peanut butter cookies. We sat down together, she on one side of the table, I on the other.

"Well," she said finally.

I wasn't responsive. I had no desire to confide in anyone today. "Well, what?"

"Elizabeth, don't be difficult. You know, and I know, that you have something on your mind. Now please tell me about it."

I waited awhile, then without any warning, I began to cry. She reached over and put her hand on mine. "Is it so terrible that you can't tell me about it? Is it Dennis?"

"It's everything!" I wailed. "It's Dennis and everything."

I told her about the party then, and how Alicia Fortunata had made me feel good, and that Dennis's parents had been really nice, but that I had just felt out of place in their world. "It wasn't because they all have plenty of money,

155

honestly, Mother, it was just that I kept thinking of how you'd have loved it, and I wished you were giving the party and that some dashing, intelligent man would sweep you off your feet and give you a life like that. I'm explaining badly, Mother, but it's not just that I was feeling sorry for myself. I want you to have a good life." I didn't add that *I* wanted a good life too, with all those things that would make me fit into Dennis's world—like Melissa did.

She came over and put her arms around me, and I could feel all that loving warmth emanating from her, and slowly I began to feel better.

"Elizabeth, I have a good life. I have four wonderful children and a roof over my head and work I love. When your father died, I thought I could never be happy again, but gradually I realized that I had to be, even if it was a different kind of happiness. I treasured you children even more, because you were part of your father and me, and you became even more precious because he wasn't here."

"But everything is such a struggle for you, Mother. I want you to have time and money to do things, like—like—I don't know. I guess like clubs and parties and trips and things."

She spread her hands wide. "Can you imagine me involved in something like a garden club? I have a garden, and I love to dig in it and grow things, but I don't want to talk about it at a club meeting. That's just not my thing, Elizabeth. I have friends, but I'm not a joiner." Her face grew more serious. "I can't deny life could be a little easier, but at least it's a challenge, and it will get easier."

I wasn't convinced. "I want it to be better *now*." So Dennis will love me *now*, I added silently.

She shrugged. "That's not the way life is, and it's just as well you learn it now as later." She was so serious, and that made me realize that usually she made a joke of things. "You know, Elizabeth, a Norman Mailer or a J.D. Salinger might not consider confession writing very important, but it's easy for me to do, it helps to earn our living, and every now and then some-one writes a letter to the editor of one of my magazines and says that my story has helped her over a bad spot in her life. And that makes it all worthwhile." The corners of her mouth curled in that funny little smile I'd inherited from her. "Besides, I have my dream—my novel. Perhaps it will never sell, but to me it seems wonderful, and I have fantasies about its be-coming a best seller and making us rich and famous!"

She poured me another cup of tea. "Eliza-beth, I wish I could make you understand one thing: material possessions are very nice to have, but you can use only so many *things* and go to so many parties and dances. Then you get bored, because the real pleasures in life are the people you love and the work you love. I know that sounds corny to you, but most of the old sentiments are corny. The thing is, they're also true."

I didn't say anything, but I was thinking of what she'd said. I have great respect for my mother's opinions. I might fight with her sometimes, but I never question her principles. I found myself wishing I could be like her and hold up my head and believe that I was equal to anyone—and that Dennis could love me even if I wasn't from his world.

The next two days at school weren't the greatest. Dennis waved at me from across the lunchroom and talked to me in history class, and I told him I'd had a great time at the party, but we didn't really *talk*. He had no basketball practice Monday and Tuesday nights, and I had baby-sitting jobs lined up for Monday and Wednesday nights, both of them on the outskirts of town, so there wasn't even the possibility of any kind of date—and I didn't think he was about to ask me for one, anyway. Probably the feeling had all been on my side, anyway, but Dennis had seemed so loving that I'd begun to hope. Now I'd stopped hoping.

Wednesday afternoon, at orchestra rehearsal, I was a little early, and Mr. Greeley called me aside. "Elizabeth, I'm sure I don't have to tell you that you have musical ability. You're too good for this orchestra." He smiled. "But don't desert us, because we need you!"

He was sitting on the piano bench, and I was perched on the edge of one of the auditorium seats. He leaned over and touched my hand. "Alicia Fortunata is a great friend of mine, and she told me last night that she had met you at a party at the Whitcombs'. She was very, very impressed with your playing and hoped I might help you along." He paused, as if choosing his words carefully. "I know your father is gone and that you might not be able to afford music lessons, but I think I have a solution."

How did he know that? I wondered, feeling angry and hurt. But of course, teachers talked with one another about their students. It was only natural.

"You say your uncle has been giving you lessons, and he must be a very good teacher indeed, because he's certainly brought out your talent. But I'm sure he'd agree you're ready for professional training now."

I said stiffly, "Yes, he tells me I'm ready to go on now—that he's taught me about all he knows."

The orchestra was tuning up now, and I saw Amy and Dennis come in and take their seats on the stage. I knew they couldn't see me very well, under the bright lights of the stage, and I was glad. Amy would be sure to ask me what Mr. Greeley had been talking about so confidentially. We do tell each other everything, but somehow I knew I wasn't going to want to tell her this.

"Miss Fortunata would like to recommend you to the board of the Hoffman School of Music. They have auditions, but I know you can pass them easily. The tuition is free, and they have some very fine teachers there. It could be the start of a wonderful career for you. What do you say?"

I tried to sound grateful, because I knew he meant to be kind, but I was humiliated. The Hoffman School was mainly for the gifted poor, and I knew it, and he knew it, and Alicia Fortunata knew it. I didn't want anybody giving me free lessons; I was too independent for that.

"I'll have to talk with my mother about it," I said finally. "Thank you very much, Mr. Greeley."

I went up to my seat then, shaking so that at first I thought I couldn't play at all. But I was angry enough to play better than ever, slashing away at the strings like a demon, performing too selfishly, too brilliantly, so that the rehearsal seemed like a showcase for me. I was ashamed afterward, but I was so uptight that it seemed the only way I could behave.

As we all trooped off the stage an hour later, Dennis stopped me for a second, his hand on my shoulder. He looked at me rather strangely. "You sounded as though you were having a

160

race with your violin today," he said. "And I think you won."

"I know I played badly," I said, my voice cold.

"It wasn't bad. It was good—too good. By the time the concert comes along, you'll have left us all behind. And you were the one who was too timid to try out for the orchestra!"

He sounded just like himself, teasing and affectionate, but I could think only of the fact that he hadn't treated me as his date at the party, that Melissa had established herself there as friend of the family, friend of Dennis.

"We're having an early dinner tonight," he said, "because my parents are going to some political party. But I'll call you later, OK?"

"You may not be able to get me," I said, "I have to baby-sit tonight. I'd better catch up with Amy now."

He held me back for a second. "Elizabeth, is something wrong? Are you mad at me?"

I pulled away. "Everything's just great," I said. "Just great."

Chapter Eighteen

Mr. Friedman picked me up at five and took me to his house in Medford. He and Mrs. Friedman were taking one of his clients out to dinner. "We won't be very late," she promised. "I know it's a school night. Did you bring your homework?"

"Yes, I'll work on it as soon as I get Robin off to bed."

"Help yourself to snacks and soft drinks from the fridge," she said, and off they went.

They were really nice people, and their three year old, Robin, was an adorable little girl with brown, curly hair and dark, laughing eyes. She never made any fuss when I put her to bed, only begging wistfully for a bedtime story to be read aloud. Tonight I read from her mother's old copy of *Peter Rabbit*, and she went off to sleep almost immediately.

I went back to the living room and started my

homework, but almost instantly I began to listen for the phone. Dennis had said he'd call me, and he always kept his word, but he didn't know where I was baby-sitting. He could call and ask Mother or Michelle, of course, but would he? After all, I hadn't been very nice to him that afternoon, and he might not be interested, anyway.

The Friedmans came back about ten, and Mr. Friedman drove me home. There was a car in front of our house, but not one I recognized. I thanked Mr. Friedman and ran up our front steps. Before I could put my hand on the knob, someone opened the door for me.

"Dennis! What are you doing here?"

The white teeth flashed, and he held the door wider. "A fine way to greet a man who has just played five hundred games of chinese checkers with your little brother Justin."

I had to laugh a little at that. "It's your own fault for buying them for him. He never even knew about chinese checkers until you dug it up!"

"Well, he's in bed now, sleeping his victory sleep, and your mother is in her study typing, and Michelle is doing her homework, and Bonita must be fast asleep. But I thought I'd wait a little while, because your mother told me you would only sit until nine or ten."

I tossed my books on the coffee table and

took off my jacket and threw it in a chair. "Is that your car outside?"

"My mother's. I told you she and my father were going to a political party of some kind. He drove, and she said I could take her car. Mine's in the garage again."

I said grudgingly, "Want some tea or some milk or something?"

"I brought two jugs of sweet cider left from the party. Let's have some of that."

We went into the kitchen, and I poured the cider, amber colored and fresh smelling as an orchard. But the mention of the party set me off again. I put out some cheese cubes and crackers and sat down opposite him. With calculated bitterness, I said, "I should think you'd have gone to Melissa's. She's part of your social world, after all. Why are you slumming tonight?"

For the first time since I'd known him, I think, I saw real anger in Dennis's beautiful eyes. "What's that supposed to mean?"

"It means your Halloween party brought me to my senses. Melissa made it very plain that she belonged there with you and your parents, while I was just part of the entertainment. And you didn't bother to make it look any different."

He grabbed my shoulders. "Listen, Elizabeth Ashton. You're worth two of Melissa and don't think I don't know it. What could I do? I couldn't leave the party to take you home, and you did have a ride with your best friend. Why was that

164

so terrible? Why are you so uptight about these things? Why not do things the most comfortable way possible?"

It made sense, but I still wanted to fight. "You certainly haven't bothered to get in touch with me since then, either."

He looked exasperated. "Oh, Elizabeth. That's silly. I thought we were comfortable enough with each other, so neither of us would feel neglected if the other one was busy. And I don't mean I was busy with another girl, either. Alicia Fortunata stayed overnight with us Saturday, and on Sunday my parents had some people in to meet her. And I've had basketball practice two nights this week. I was just busy, and I thought you were, too."

Feeling sulky, I took another swig of the cider. "I have been." Then, no longer caring what he thought, I added, "Mr. Greeley wants me to audition for the Hoffman School. He thinks I might get a scholarship to study violin."

His face lit up. "That's great! You're going to do it, aren't you?"

I shrugged. "I might. But it seems like charity to me. Your friend Miss Fortunata recommended me, by the way."

"Look," he said sternly, "there's no charity about it. You have a great talent, and it's your right to get training. Look at all the grants people get in order to paint pictures and write poetry and sing. You have to do it, Elizabeth."

165

Suddenly he stood up. "Get your jacket. I want to sit out on your back porch. I love your back porch, Elizabeth. We don't have one."

Of course I went outside with him, despite my best resolutions, and we sat very close together on the steps in the moonlight. For a long time we hardly said anything, just stared out at the grass, which had turned silver in the moonlight, and at the tall sunflowers, which my mother had planted for the birds. Two of the cats—Figaro and Betsy—appeared out of the shadows, out of nowhere, materializing like little after-Halloween ghosts. They sat on either side of us, and Figaro rubbed his gray head on Dennis's leg.

Dennis stroked the cat's head gently and said, "I'm very flattered, you know. I think Figaro really likes me."

"He does." And I like you, too, Dennis Whitcomb, I thought. I love you, but I don't want to.

As though he'd heard my unspoken thought, Dennis suddenly drew my face close to his and kissed me as he had that day at the red brick house. "I'm falling in love with you, Elizabeth Ashton," he said. "I've tried not to, but I am."

"I think I fell in love with you that first night," I whispered. "But I always have the feeling you're staying away from me."

"That's because I am. I told you, I shouldn't have a steady girl, not for years, but I can't help it. Will you be my girl, Elizabeth? You know I

166

have years of school, and you have years of study so you can become a famous violinist. Do you think we can make it together, keep things under control?"

"I think so," I said. Then I realized what he'd said. "But I'm not sure I want to be a violinist, Dennis. I've told you that I don't think I have the guts to make sacrifices, the way my mother and father did all those years. The way Mother still does."

He pulled away then, to look into my eyes. In the pale, silver light, his eyes were like cats' eyes—deep and mysterious. "Listen, do you want to know what I think of your mother—and your father, too, because he must have been a great guy? I think your family is terrific, and that means your mother especially. They're real, Elizabeth. Lots of the people I know aren't. I don't mean my parents. They've got their feet on the ground because they've worked hard. But some of the people we know, like Melissa and her parents, are phonies. They think money is everything, but I know it's not."

He kissed me again, and for a while I forgot everything. I could think only of how wonderful it was to be in his arms, to feel our bodies so close that they were like one body. In the back of my mind, something told me Dennis was right. It would be hard to wait out the years. And with that thought, I knew I was committed. I would audition for the Hoffman School, I would thrust all my energy and intelligence into my music. Anything less would be to deny my father and my mother. And Dennis.

After awhile he just sat there with his hand holding mine, gently and sweetly. "Remember the day we first went to my grandparents' house?"

"Of course."

His cheek was against mine now. "I told you then that I planned to live there some day. Well, now I know it won't be alone. Now I know it will be with a girl in a long dress, a girl who will stand there in front of the fireplace and make beautiful music on her violin."

Mother had said it was important to have a dream, and now I knew she was right. I had something to look forward to, something to work toward. And although it's a dream now, one day it will be real. I can hardly wait!

Read these great new
Sweet Dreams romances

#13 THE SUMMER JENNY FELL IN LOVE by Barbara Conklin (#20789-x • $1.95)

Jenny's summer gets off to a bad start when seventeen-year-old Cliff and his mother become the new boarders. Even though they both try hard, Jenny and Cliff just can't get along. But when Cliff starts interfering with Jenny's love life, she realizes it's because he is jealous. Suddenly, something totally unexpected is happening with Jenny's summer.

#14 DANCE OF LOVE by Jocelyn Saal (#20790-3 • $1.95)

Ever since third grade, Polly and Jennifer have shared everything from ballet lessons to boy talk to their dreams of becoming famous dancers. Then Polly meets Cott Townsend, and her plans—and her friendship with Jennifer—get turned upside down.

#15 THINKING OF YOU by Jeanette Nobile (#2516-2 • $1.95)

Fran's tired of being called a "brain"...and missing all the fun! She wants to go to parties, have dates and fall in love, but can she change her image just a little and still be herself?

#16 HOW DO YOU SAY GOODBYE by Margaret Burman (#22517-0 • $1.95)

Lisa wants to break up with Lawrence, but she's afraid she'll hurt his feelings. But she really likes going out with Alex. So Lisa lives a double life of lies and confusion—until the night when her lies go too far.

#17 ASK ANNIE by Suzanne Rand
(#22518-9 • $1.95)

At first, Annie was thrilled to give Tim advice about his girlfriend—until he asks Annie how to keep beautiful, stuck-up Marcy in line. If she helps Tim keep Marcy, Annie will never get a chance with him. But if she doesn't, will Tim stop being her friend?

#18 TEN-BOY SUMMER by Janet Quin-Harkin
(#22519-7 • $1.95)

Jill's vacation gets off to a wild start when her best friend, Toni, thinks up a contest—who can be the first to date ten new boys! It seems like a great idea until Jill meets Craig and knows she's in love. If Jill drops out of the contest, she won't be able to face her best friend. If she doesn't, she'll lose Craig forever.

And make sure to look for these Sweet Dreams romances, coming soon:

Read all of these Sweet Dreams romances, on sale now wherever Bantam paperbacks are sold or order directly from Bantam Books by including $1.00 to cover postage and handling and sending a check to Bantam Books, Dept. 503, 414 East Golf Road, Des Plaines, Ill. 60016. Allow 4-6 weeks for delivery. This offer expires 1/83.